He couldn't help the grin then, but he refrained from comment.

Now that the drama was over, he could finally breathe. His heart was only now resuming its normal rhythm. Hearing Jenny's scream had sent adrenaline rushing through him in a torrent. Holding her in his arms hadn't helped much, either. It was going to be some time before those lingering memories would fade. Even now, the soft scent of jasmine she used remained in his mind.

He slowly wandered around the cabin noting the changes she had made. He raked his hands through his hair, sighing, and glanced her way. "You're really going through with it. You're really going to stay here."

He saw her tense.

She contemplated him through narrowed eyes. "What are you doing here anyway? If you came to talk me out of my ranch, you can just leave again."

When he took a step toward her she hastily removed herself to the other side of the room, placing the sofa between them. She glared at him warily, and his aggravation mounted.

"Look. I don't know what you have against me, but I'm not the big bad ogre you make me out to be."

Books by Darlene Mindrup

Love Inspired Heartsong Presents

There's Always Tomorrow
Love's Pardon
Beloved Protector

DARLENE MINDRUP

has always had a love of writing and an active imagination. Years of journalism classes and homeschooling her children gave her the tools to make her writing better and more professional (and with fewer errors). She has a love of history that comes through in her novels, especially Bible history and World War II.

DARLENE MINDRUP

The Rancher Next Door

HEARTSONG
PRESENTS

Recycling programs
for this product may
not exist in your area.

LOVE INSPIRED BOOKS

ISBN-13: 978-0-373-48714-1

THE RANCHER NEXT DOOR

www.Harlequin.com

Printed in U.S.A.

The heavens declare the glory of God;
the skies proclaim the work of his hands.
—*Psalms* 19:1

To Allen and Dena who believed in this story
even when I didn't.

Chapter 1

Jenny Gordon took one look at her new home and sighed. She should have known it was too good to be true.

"Oh, Jen! We can't possibly live here!"

The wailing voice of her younger sister brought Jenny Gordon out of her stupor of shock. She stared somberly around at her morose surroundings. Dirt and dust met her inspection whichever way she turned. At first the little cabin left to her by a distant cousin had seemed to be the answer to prayer, but the reality was different from the dream....

"Jen?" Jenny turned to her younger brother, David. His twin sister, Renee, was still sniffling from the doorway, trying desperately to hold back tears.

"Jen? What are we going to do?" He stared disdainfully around the rough-looking log cabin, lips set in a grim line. "We can't live here."

Jenny cast him a fleeting smile. Whatever her own thoughts were, she must keep from her brother and sister the extent of her worry. "Oh, I don't know, David. It's not so bad."

His dark eyebrows went swiftly toward his curling black hair and as swiftly lowered to meet in a straight line across his forehead. Blue eyes snapped with anger.

"Are you out of your ever-loving mind!"

"Oh, Jen, no!" Renee's shocked voice mingled with her brother's irate one.

Jenny lifted a shaking hand to her head and pushed her ash-brown hair from her eyes, which felt dulled by fatigue and worry. It had taken almost everything they'd had in savings to get here, and now she was faced with a definite dilemma.

After her parents had died in an accident shortly after their move to New York from North Dakota, Jenny had hurried home from the university to care for the twins. The comfortable living she had been used to had ceased to exist when the estate was finally settled. Poor investments and estate fees had put on hold any possibility of receiving an inheritance from her parents' insurance policies.

It hadn't helped that the only job she'd been able to find was as a waitress in a greasy diner on the corner close to where they had found a cheap apartment, and she had had to leave the twins on their own for much of the time. The hours had been long, the pay a mere pittance, but it had helped to tide them over until she could find something a little more permanent. Except nothing permanent had ever come.

Just when Jenny had about reached the end of her endurance, the letter had arrived from the lawyer's office. Jenny could barely remember Father talking about a cousin who had come to live with his family when he was just a boy. He had left when he was twenty-one and had written Father periodically, but Jenny hadn't thought of him in years. She had been amazed when she'd received the letter from the lawyer's office about inheriting Cousin Tito's property.

And now here they were in the little Arizona cabin that was nothing like the home she had envisioned.

Jenny was brought back to the present by the squeaking of the floor as David shifted his suitcase and placed it in front of him. There was a defiant set to his shoulders.

"Jen, this place isn't fit for a pig much less a human." He kicked some dust under his feet, causing little dust motes to dance through the sunlight spilling in the open door. "What are we gonna do? We sure can't stay here."

For the first time Jenny fully took stock of her surroundings. After the first shock had worn off, she noticed that the cabin was not really a cabin in the rough sense of the word. It was actually a five-room structure made to look like a cabin. There were two bedrooms, a kitchen and dining room combined, a small bathroom and the small living room in which they were presently standing. Sheets were draped over much of the furniture, giving the rooms an eerie quality in the dim light.

The building itself was solidly built and what had appeared to be deterioration was really neglect. An air of loneliness seemed to permeate the place, calling out to the isolation Jenny had been feeling since the death of her parents. Despite its flaws, it was as though the place was calling her home.

Jenny shook herself from her fanciful imaginings and focused on the reality of the situation. On closer inspection she could see things she hadn't noticed before. Light switches were evidence that the cabin had electricity. The kitchen had a sink and a refrigerator, and a small stove stood against the wall in the corner. That the cabin was already furnished was a major blessing, considering they had no furniture of their own. Jenny felt somewhat cheered by these details—until she looked at her siblings.

Renee had returned to the porch and refused to come back into the house. Her ramrod-straight back gave mute testimony to the tension and anger she was feeling. David gave Jenny one final disgusted look and joined his twin on the porch. He seated himself on the stairs at the side of the porch, away from Jen's scrutiny. If looks could kill, David's final glare would have sent her to her grave.

Jenny sighed and turned to the bathroom. When they had entered she had only given it a cursory inspection. Now she took the time to look around her. A white-enamel claw-foot tub was in the farthest corner. A small commode was in the other corner and a white-enamel basin stood between. The three items took up most of the space and left little room for anything else. A window above the sink let in a pale, sickly light through the brown grime. One pane was busted out in the corner. The thought that it might have been vandals disturbed her, but she pushed the alarming feelings aside.

As Jenny continued her inspection, a resolve was forming in her mind. This cabin was solidly built. There was obviously electricity and running water. If she and the twins were to clean it up there was no reason that they couldn't live here. She was beginning to get excited at the prospect. Could they do it? What other choice did they have? There was no money left to return to New York and nowhere to return to if they did. There might be some money coming from Cousin Tito's estate eventually, but that would take time and they needed somewhere to live now.

With grim resolve Jenny went outside. She straightened her shoulders as though she were preparing for battle, as in a sense she knew that she was.

"David. Renee. I have something to say." She watched David stiffen. Renee turned to her expectantly, her tear-streaked face looking hopefully toward Jenny.

"I think," Jenny began, "that with a little work we could manage to live here."

David spun around on the porch. Renee's mouth dropped open.

"Wha—?"

Jenny raised both hands in the air. "Just listen to me a minute."

A mulish expression settled over David's features. His very posture spoke of open defiance, but the thought of the tenement houses in New York and David's descent into an association with the lower dregs of society spurred her on. If there was any way possible, they would never live that way again.

"Maybe you didn't notice that there is electricity and water in the cabin," she told them hopefully, pausing and looking around. "At least there will be when we have it turned on. And there's a refrigerator in the kitchen and a stove. There's even a tub and commode in the bathroom."

The excitement she was beginning to feel came through in her voice.

"The place is a pigsty, for crying out loud! You can't possibly be serious. It would take ages to make this place livable! Where would we live in the meantime?" David placed an arm around Renee's shoulders. "I don't want my sisters living in a place like this."

Jenny stared hard at him until he eventually looked down in embarrassment.

"Have you forgotten how we've been living for the past few years?" She waved her hand around. "This is paradise by comparison."

Renee glanced at her brother and Jenny could see the thoughts flitting across her face. Renee's concern for her twin was equal to her own. If they didn't do something soon, they were going to lose him. They shared a look over his head. Renee lifted her chin, her blue eyes shining luminously. "If you think it's best, Jen, then I'm willing to give it a go."

David's arm dropped from her shoulders as though he had just been stung. He glared from one to the other. "I can't believe it! I can't believe my ears!" He sounded almost desperate.

Jenny lowered her voice, unconsciously pleading with her brother. "David, we all need to work together." She reached a hand toward him but he jerked away. His voice vibrated with his wrath.

"I'll help! You bet I'll help! And as soon as I help you make this place livable, I'm outta here. Do you hear me!"

He flung himself off the porch and stumbled across the yard toward the desert. Jenny started to go after him but Renee placed a restraining hand against her arm. "Let him go, Jenny. He needs time to take it all in."

No one knew David better than his twin so Jenny reluctantly bowed to her wisdom. Jenny worriedly watched as David became a small dot in the distance. "He might get hurt."

"He won't go far." With that pronouncement Renee turned and went through the front door of the cabin. Jenny followed her, shoulders drooping wearily. She knew that David wouldn't make this easy, but would he really run away? It would take all of them working together to pull this off, but David was so impulsive, there was no telling what he might do.

Inside, the cabin seemed cooler, a blessed relief from the sweltering heat outside. Renee had stopped and was staring gloomily around her.

"Do you really think we can fix this place up? And where do we get the money to do it?" She looked inquiringly over her shoulder at Jenny.

Jenny sighed heavily. They still had a little money left in the bank, but not much. She looked hopelessly around her. "I guess the first thing we need to do is have the lights and water turned on. Mrs. Ames said she would stop back for us at one o'clock. We can talk to her about it then." She glanced at her watch. "That's still thirty minutes away."

When they had arrived in Phoenix, they had been met at the airport by Hattie Ames, the wife of Jacob Ames, the lawyer who had handled Cousin Tito's estate. Mrs. Ames was a tall woman with slightly graying dark hair coiled into a bun on her neck. She'd been wearing an elegant burgundy two-piece skirt and jacket with a pink chiffon blouse, leaving Jenny feeling dowdy in comparison. Her old jeans were showing definite signs of wear and her faded T-shirt didn't fare much better.

Jenny had to envy Hattie's seeming imperviousness to the sweltering July heat that had Jenny dripping with perspiration. The hour-and-a-half drive to Mayer had seemed endless despite the air-conditioned comfort of the car.

Jenny went to the door and leaned against the frame. The desert landscape shimmered as the heat reflected off the hot sand. A large bird circled overhead and she shivered as she recognized the predatory buzzard. Where was David? He had to be back before Mrs. Ames returned.

Renee walked up behind her and laid her chin on Jenny's shoulder. Perspiration glistened on her face. Jenny was surprised to discover that Renee was almost as tall as she now. She glanced sideways at her younger sister, taking in the softness of her face. Renee's black hair glistened vibrantly. She was so lovely, even at twelve. Jenny felt a quick pang of envy but just as quickly snuffed it out. Ugly memories that she had thought were in the past struggled to rear their dark heads.

"I could sure go for a cold soda about now," Renee remarked, interrupting those thoughts and scattering them to the far winds.

Jenny smiled. "I'd settle for anything to drink. My throat feels as though it has a layer of cotton in it."

Renee stepped up beside her sister and squinted, her focus down the dirt road that led to Cousin Tito's ranch. Following her gaze, Jenny saw a vehicle rapidly approaching. She glanced at her watch.

"Heavens. Mrs. Ames is early. Renee, go see if you can find David. I don't want to keep her waiting. Not in this heat."

"I couldn't agree more!" Renee swiftly descended the stairs and went in the direction they had last seen David disappearing.

Jenny walked along the porch and rested a jeans-clad hip against the rail. Arms crossed, she watched the rapidly approaching car. A smile quirked her lips. Mrs. Ames must be in a mighty big hurry.

It was only seconds before Jenny realized that the vehicle didn't belong to Mrs. Ames. Her car was a white Lincoln Town Car. This was some sort of truck. Jenny's eyebrows pulled together and she waited in silent anticipation.

A dark blue Jeep Cherokee slid to a halt in front of her. Almost before the car stopped, the front driver's door was thrown open and a large, blond-haired giant fairly threw himself from the vehicle. He strode toward her, taking the porch steps two at a time.

"Who in thunder are you and what are you doing here? This is private property!"

Jenny stared up into blazing green eyes, her heart rate accelerating at the intimidating picture the man made. Never had she seen such an earthy shade of green in a set of eyes before. Nostrils flaring, the man reminded her of stories of avenging Vikings of long ago, especially with a day's growth of whiskers shadowing his firm jaw. She shivered despite the sweltering heat.

"Well?" The belligerence of his tone released her from the daze his fiery presence had induced. She felt the hackles rise on the back of her neck at his arrogance. She drew herself to her full five-foot-six-inch height, which still left her a good eight inches shorter than he was.

"Look, Mr. Whoever-you-are, exactly what right do you have to question *me?*"

Green eyes locked with blue. Invisible sparks seemed to pass between them, the atmosphere crackling with imperceptible energy. They stared at each other for what felt to

Jenny like an eon. The air seemed to grow thicker around them and Jenny found it hard to breathe, her mouth growing even dryer than before, and she knew it had absolutely nothing to do with the Arizona heat. She willed herself to look away, but her eyes had a mind of their own.

"Jen?"

Jenny finally dragged her gaze away from the man and focused on David standing behind him. She tried to settle the rapid beating of her heart. The stranger had swung around at the sound of David's voice. His eyes went from David to Renee, who was standing slightly behind her brother, and back to Jenny again.

"What in thunder is going on here? A pack of runaways no doubt." The stranger's lip curled disdainfully. His eyes slid over the three of them as if they were some kind of dirty vagrants and David squirmed slightly under that intense regard.

"Well, you can just pack it up and go back home where you belong. You're not staying here."

"You can't tell us what to do!" David flung himself forward and stubbornly faced the stranger, his trembling lip giving lie to his bravado.

Jenny didn't appreciate the stranger's overbearing attitude. Although she was proud of her brother's attempt at being their protector, it suddenly occurred to her how very alone they were out here and that this man could possibly be dangerous. He certainly looked as if he was capable of violence. Muscles rippled across broad shoulders as the stranger pulled his Stetson from his head and shifted it from one hand to the other. David quailed under his look and Jenny was suffering severe misgivings about tangling with such an individual. From somewhere deep inside she pulled on reserves of courage and decided her best defense would be a quick counterattack.

"David, be still," Jenny told him quietly. She stepped forward, pushed her brother to the side out of harm's way and turned to the man. "Perhaps you would explain yourself."

His green eyes fired afresh. "*You* want *me* to explain *myself!* You've got a lot of nerve, lady! I happen to be looking after this place for someone and that gives me the right to question *you,* and I have no intention of explaining myself to a bunch of kids."

Of all the supercilious attitudes! Anger that had been squelched by fright now pummeled its way to the surface. "I'll have you know that I am not a child!"

His eyes took a slow inspection of her, making her flinch under his appraisal. Jenny squirmed under that scathing look, knowing that she didn't look her best. With her hair in a ponytail and no makeup, she probably did look like the child he accused her of being. The fact that she was thin didn't help matters, either. She was not exactly an imposing figure.

When his gaze connected with hers again, something had altered almost imperceptibly in his hard stare and she unwillingly responded to it.

Those memories she had tried so hard to bury now rose to the surface. Her first year of college she had met Alexander. Having been sheltered all her life, she'd been easy prey for the likes of such a practiced charmer. They had dated for a short time and she had thought herself in love. She had been devastated when she'd overheard a conversation between him and his buddies in which he'd explained that he could overlook Jenny's lack of looks as long as he knew she had plenty of money.

He had dropped her like a hot potato after her parents died and he realized that there would be no big inheritance coming from the estate. It had shattered her faith in herself. Although the hurt from that rejection had diminished over the years, all of those insecurities came rushing back to haunt her now. This man exuded that same kind of magnetism.

Despite his towering rage and her own rising anger, Jenny could feel the tug of his attraction. Surprised that she was so affected, she slid her hands into the back pockets of her jeans and frowned up at him, exasperated with herself. What was there about the man that shortened her breath and muddled her thinking? In her whole twenty-six years of existence she had never been as affected by a man as she was by this one. Even her feelings for Alexander paled in comparison, making her more leery than ever.

Their standoff lasted several long seconds before Jenny finally capitulated.

"Fine," she told him. "My name is Jenny Gordon. This is my brother, David, and my sister, Renee. And this—" she moved her hand in a sweeping gesture "—is our ranch." She dropped the bomb casually and waited for his reaction. She hadn't long to wait.

"In a pig's eye!"

Mitch Anderson stared in openmouthed amazement at the three belligerent faces regarding him as though *he* were the interloper. He had seen someone on Tito's porch upon his return from town and, having been the recent target of juvenile vandalism, was not in a particularly forthcoming mood.

Wherever had these kids gotten the idea that this property belonged to them? Hopefully they weren't the targets of some sort of scam. The one named Jenny looked as though a good puff of wind would blow her away. Looking at her now, he could see that she was older than he had at first assumed. She was neither homely nor cute, but something about her arrested his attention. Those wide sapphire eyes regarding him with such open hostility held the faintest look of desperation. Opening his mouth to deny their claim, he felt as though he was about to kick a wounded puppy.

"It's true," the boy piped up, interrupting what he was

about to say while a female replica of him settled for a vigorous nod of the head.

Before he could reply he heard the sound of another vehicle barreling down the dirt road. Dust billowed out behind it. As if in silent agreement all four figures waited for the car to arrive. Hattie Ames's Town Car parked tidily behind his Jeep. She slowly emerged from the car, a wide smile on her face. He had no idea what she was doing here, but he had a sudden premonition that settled a hard lump in his stomach.

"Mitch! How nice. I see you've met your new neighbors."

The lump in his stomach grew to alarming proportions. Incredulity, anger, frustration were only a few of the myriad emotions churning their way through his gut before he forced himself to calm down. He turned to Jenny, his eyes slowly traveling from the tip of her mousy head to the toes of her running shoes and back again. *You have got to be kidding!*

When his eyes connected with her flashing blue ones, he could tell that his reservations were evident on his face. Each time he got caught by that look, it was as though some sort of magnetic pull was dragging him outside of himself. He frowned, berating himself for his foolish reaction. He said nothing, waiting until Hattie joined them on the porch.

Arching an eyebrow, Jenny turned toward Hattie. "Mitch?" she queried.

Looking puzzled, Hattie glanced from Jenny to Mitch. "Didn't you introduce yourselves?"

"We hadn't gotten around to it yet," Mitch told her drily.

"Oh." Hattie glanced curiously from one to the other. "Mitch owns the ranch west of here." She gestured in the direction that was evidently west. "There are actually very few cattle ranches left anymore. Mitch's is one of the few prosperous ones still around."

David's eyes widened. "Are you a *real* cowboy?" He

was obviously impressed, seemingly forgetting his earlier animosity.

"If you mean do I ride around on a horse all day singing cattle songs and eating from a chuck wagon the way they do in the movies, then no, I'm not a cowboy." He suddenly flashed a smile and, despite his chaotic feelings, felt himself softening toward the boy. "Is that what you meant?"

The boy's face flushed but he was undeterred. "Yeah, I guess that is what I thought."

"I raise cattle for beef," he told him. "We do ride horses and round up our cattle, but nothing like the old days."

A sudden silence descended on the group.

Hattie hastily stepped forward, eyes darting perplexedly from him to Jenny. She was obviously aware of the thick, almost oppressive, atmosphere.

"Well, now, what have you decided?" At Jenny's questioning look, she gestured around. "I mean, if you want to sell this place I'm sure I could find a buyer for you."

"Really?" David and Renee chimed together.

Hattie smiled at them. "Really." She turned to Mitch. "As a matter of fact, Mitch here's wanted this place for a while now. Isn't that right, Mitch?"

He willed the belligerence from his voice before he answered. "I will make you a good offer," he told Jenny, caught once again by the desperate look in her eyes. He held his breath, waiting for her answer.

Jenny glanced around her, trying to ignore the hopeful looks on her siblings' faces. The buzzard she had seen earlier was a mere speck in the bright azure sky. The stillness of the hot afternoon settled around her and she felt herself relax for the first time in weeks. What was it about this place that made her feel so at peace?

Periodically she could hear a bird trilling close by or the wind skipping a tumbleweed across the sandy terrain. One could almost feel the presence of God here, which astonished her, because she hadn't given much thought to Him for some time.

"It's not for sale." Jenny heard her own voice with some surprise. She was fairly certain that that wasn't what she had meant to say. There was so much to consider, not the least of which was how they would survive until she could get a job.

She ignored the swift intake of breath from her siblings.

Mitch's lips formed a tight, thin line. "You haven't even heard my offer yet. I'm willing to pay you considerably more than the ranch is worth."

Jenny looked him squarely in the eyes. For once in her life she had no doubts. This was home. She could feel it. How could it be that she seemed to fit right into this rugged landscape? And what of Renee and David? Her heart gave a frightened lurch. Was she doing right by the twins? Was she being selfish? She had to do what she thought was best, and in her heart she felt this was the right decision, though she didn't understand why.

Mrs. Ames cleared her throat. "Perhaps you want to think it over?"

Jenny shook her head. "No, Mrs. Ames. I definitely don't want to sell. I want us to live here."

David flung himself away and stomped off to the other end of the porch and Renee let out a small sigh. Mitch Anderson snorted in disbelief.

"Do you have any idea what it's like out here? This is no place for a woman alone with two kids. There are things you need to take into consideration."

That was certainly true enough, not the least of which was a means of transportation. If she had to rent a car that would definitely cut into the little money they had in their savings. Still, something told her this was where she was meant to be. Normally a more logical person with a sound sense of judgment, she ignored the tiny voice that warned her against making snap decisions.

"Regardless, I intend to stay."

His narrowed green-eyed gaze seemed to question her sanity. He slammed his Stetson on his head and went to turn away. He paused a moment before adding, "If you change your mind, Hattie here knows how to get in touch with me." He nodded his head toward Mrs. Ames.

Jenny watched as he leaped into his Jeep before throwing it into gear and, making a U-turn, roared back down the road from whence he had made his incredible appearance. Jenny blew out a relieved breath.

"What a hunk!"

Jenny gave her sister a telling look. "That's crude, Renee," she said in rebuke, even though mentally she had to agree with her. The man was certainly handsome in a rugged sort of way. He was what her father would have called a man's man.

Mrs. Ames smiled mysteriously. "Land sakes, I've never seen Mitch so wrought up." She glanced at Jenny speculatively. "So what do *you* think of the area's most eligible bachelor?"

What did she think? Jenny mused. He was rude, arrogant, insufferable and a few other adjectives she couldn't put a name to. Still, since he was a friend of Hattie's she closed her mouth on the vitriolic words begging for release. She shook her head. "I don't know. I've just met him, haven't I?"

Still, she couldn't keep her look from following the fast-disappearing Jeep.

Hattie Ames smiled as if at some secret joke. She gave a slight chuckle. "'God works in mysterious ways,'" she quoted softly. Jenny glanced at her uneasily, wondering just exactly what she meant by that.

Chapter 2

Jenny marveled at the change in Hattie Ames as she sat beside her several hours later. The tall, stately Realtor had shed her elegant image in favor of a faded pair of jeans and an old khaki button-up shirt. A pair of tennis shoes replaced the high heels she'd worn earlier, and a ponytail bobbed from behind her head. It was hard to believe she was the same person.

She really liked Hattie Ames. There was no pretense about her. She was natural, with a spontaneous friendliness that reached out to others.

Jenny glanced out the window of the car, watching the desert flash by. Could it only have been a couple of hours since they had arrived here? It felt more like an eternity.

Hattie had taken charge and before Jenny had known what was happening she had been whisked to various offices and had spent some of her dwindling savings having the electricity and water turned on. She had tried to protest. She'd felt ill at ease bothering Hattie with her problems, but Hattie had waved away all objections.

"I'd like to be your friend. You look as though you could use one." A smile took any censure from the words and Jenny had relaxed. The forty-year-old Realtor reminded her of her own mother. Her kindness and generosity to others seemed to be an innate part of her makeup, making Jenny feel even better about her decision to stay here.

"Tito would be pleased to know that his home was being occupied again. Especially since it's you doing the occupying."

"You sound as though you knew my father's cousin."

Hattie glanced at her in surprise. "I did. We went to the same church." She shifted her eyes back to the road. "Didn't you know Tito at all?"

Jenny shook her head. "No. Father never talked much about him. I don't think they corresponded very often."

Hattie smiled. "I'm not surprised. He wasn't much for letter writing and never took to emailing, either. Didn't leave home very often." Her voice lowered. "He was a good man, though. He had a very large heart."

Jenny considered this remark. Hattie and Cousin Tito must have been very good friends. Suddenly she felt a desire to know more about this cousin who had so generously left her father his belongings. "Why did he leave everything to my father when they hadn't seen each other for years?" she asked Hattie.

Hattie paused, as though groping for words. "Well, your cousin often said that your father was responsible for saving his life. Not in the physical sense of the word." She hesitated. "Do you understand what I mean?"

Jenny nodded and waited for Hattie to continue. It was several seconds before she went on.

"Tito always wanted to do something for your father to show his appreciation. He claimed that your father's farm saved his life, but the desert saved his soul. I think he wanted the same for your father. He loved your father very much. When they were younger they were inseparable buddies." A slow reminiscent smile curved her lips. "The stories he used to tell!"

Jenny was intrigued. "Such as?"

"Oh, just little-boy escapades. It seems your father and his cousin had a penchant for being in the wrong place at the wrong time." She paused and Jenny was reminded of her father's accident. It had occurred when he had taken a shortcut en route to a conference. A truck had overturned on the icy road ahead and Jenny's father had been unable to avoid hitting it. Her parents had been killed instantly. If he hadn't taken the shortcut, they might be alive today.

Jenny stared out the window, her mind suddenly blank. Hattie had made the turn to the ranch, the cabin looking small in the distance. "Mrs. Ames, I want to thank you again for all that you've done for us."

A delicate snort followed these words and Jenny had to smile.

"It's the least I could do. I had nothing pressing today, anyway, so I might as well be useful to someone. And by the way, my name's Hattie, as Mitch told you. As everyone is always saying, Mrs. Ames is my mother-in-law."

The car pulled to a stop in front of the cabin and Jenny got out and was instantly hit with heat like a blast from a furnace. Despite the soaring temperatures of the early morning hours, the house seemed to reach out and welcome her, enveloping her in a sense of security. What had Cousin Tito found here? Did he also feel the peace that echoed through the landscape? What had he meant when he'd said that the desert had saved his soul?

Hattie was lifting supplies from the trunk. Boxes and buckets were followed by a broom and a mop. Jenny shook her head ruefully. "I appreciate you letting Renee and David stay with your son Mark. I don't think they are quite ready for this. Maybe they'll be more amenable after we've taken off some of the dirt."

Hattie set a box of cleaning supplies on the porch and

looked around her. "This is really a nice place—it's just been sitting idle too long. All it needs is a little sprucing up." She grinned at Jenny. "And maybe a woman's touch."

Jenny raised an eyebrow. "I wish I had as much faith!"

Hattie smiled softly. "Like a grain of mustard seed." At Jenny's puzzled look Hattie stood. "Shall we get started? The sun doesn't go down till around eight o'clock, but we have a lot to do before then. Let's see if the power people have been here yet."

Jenny followed Hattie into the cabin. Hattie had informed her that water was supplied from a well with a pump that was located behind the house. To have water, they first needed to have electricity.

Hattie went first to the kitchen and set the supplies on the counter by the sink. Opening the refrigerator, she placed several cans of cola on the top shelf. She then turned on the tap and water flowed freely into the bowl of the sink. Obviously the power people had been here and done their job.

She looked slowly around her. "Whew! We've certainly got our work cut out for us. Where do you want to start?"

Jenny thought for a moment. "How about if we start with the bedrooms? Then at least we'll have someplace clean to stay the night. Renee and David can help me with the rest later."

"Sounds like a good plan to me. Why don't you take one bedroom and I'll take the other, that way we can get it done faster."

Jenny agreed. When she entered the smaller of the two bedrooms, since Hattie had insisted on the larger, she was conscious of having not really seen it before. The room was furnished with a single bed, a chest of drawers and a small writing desk. This room would be perfect for David. The larger bedroom had a double bed, and she and Renee would have to share it. This was no problem; they had been sharing a room for some time now. Since their apartment had only had one bedroom, David had been forced to sleep on the sofa in the living room. To Jenny, this was an improvement.

She took down the dusty brown curtains hanging at the room's only window. The sudden presence of light lifted her spirits considerably and she determined that one of the first things she would do after they were settled somewhat would be to make bright, cheerful curtains for all the rooms.

She gingerly picked up the rug and, with the curtains, marched outside, dumping them over the porch rail. She slapped her hands together to remove the dust and paused to admire the scenery. Everything looked brown and bare except for the green prickly pear cactus dotting the landscape. Tumbleweeds rolled gently across the sand. Perhaps most people would call it desolate, but Jenny could see the beauty everywhere she turned. Shifting patterns of sand gave an eerie movability to the terrain and the sky was so blue it almost hurt the eyes.

Hattie peeked around the door. "By the way, do you happen to have any sheets and such to make up your beds?"

Jenny turned and went past her into the house. "We have some, but they won't arrive until tomorrow. I hadn't thought about it. I'm not really very prepared to stay out here, am I?"

"Well, don't let it worry you. I have some you can borrow until yours arrive."

They returned to their respective rooms and Jenny could hear Hattie softly humming to herself. Jenny recognized the hymn and stopped to listen. Hattie had a beautiful voice and the hymn reminded her of the days when she had gone to church with her parents. Those had been happy times.... She pushed away the feelings of sadness that were trying to overtake her once again.

Various noises indicated that Hattie was well on her way to having her part done, so Jenny hurried to complete her tasks, as well. Having removed the curtains and rug she was now able to clean the window, sweep the floor and dust the furniture. Scrubbing was a must, she decided, and a definite priority.

An hour later Hattie came into the room where Jenny was still on her knees scrubbing. "How about a cool drink? I could use a break."

Sweat beaded the other woman's brow; her shirt was dampened with perspiration. As the day grew progressively hotter, the little cabin was becoming stifling. Since Hattie had told her there was no air-conditioning, fans would have to be a first priority.

Jenny slowly rose to her feet, one hand pushing against the small of her back. The perspiration trickled down her spine in rivulets. "You don't have to ask me twice." She smiled ruefully. "I think I'm getting old."

Hattie laughed, the sound echoing merrily through the room. "Just remember, you're only as old as you feel."

Entering the kitchen behind her, Jenny grimaced. "Then I must be at least ninety-nine."

Still smiling, Hattie poked her head into the little refrigerator, which Jenny was thrilled to find worked. "Diet or regular?" Hattie looked around at Jenny. "Forget I asked," she remarked, handing Jenny a regular cola. "I know it's fashionable to be thin, but aren't you overdoing it just a tad?"

Too embarrassed to explain their impoverished circumstances, Jenny remained silent.

They sat at the table that was nestled snugly in the corner of the kitchen. Four chairs surrounded it, remarkably sturdy. All the furniture seemed to be hewed from raw wood. When Jenny commented upon it, excitement sparkled in Hattie's eyes. "Tito loved working with wood. He even built this cabin himself." She surveyed the cabin and its interior. "The cabin was actually a kit that he purchased in Phoenix. They're quite popular here. He made most of the furniture in this cabin. Let me show you my favorite."

Jenny followed her into the living room and watched as Hattie began pulling covers from the furniture. Lovingly she slid her hands over the surface of a rustic table sitting in front of the couch. The top seemed to be made of some sort of stone.

"This is shale, a natural stone found north of here. Mitch brought it back with him from Flagstaff and Tito decided it would make a perfect tabletop."

Jenny marveled at the beauty of the piece. Why hadn't she taken the time to look more closely? Now she noticed several things she had missed before. The tables and chairs were made from carved wood and stone, beautiful in their simplicity. Jenny remarked upon the uniqueness of the end tables gracing each side of the sofa.

Hattie wrinkled her nose. "I'm not sure I should tell you about those."

"Why?" Jenny's curiosity was aroused.

"Mitch and Tito went elk hunting one fall." Hattie pointed to the tables in question. "Those are the horns from their kill." She watched Jenny's face and was rewarded with a puckered frown.

"Ugh! You mean those are the horns of a dead animal?"

Hattie nodded solemnly, her eyes sparkling with suppressed merriment.

Jenny headed back to the kitchen, throwing Hattie a disgusted look over her shoulder.

Several hours later they were headed back to town. Hattie pointed out the road to Mitch's ranch as they passed and Jenny frowned. The troublesome man had been in and out of her thoughts all afternoon. She turned her eyes back to the road ahead, refusing to give Hattie the satisfaction of seeing her interest.

Dusk was descending and with it the desert blossomed into color from the setting sun. Jenny was awed by the colorful panorama spreading out in front of her eyes. Vivid hues of orange, red, yellow and purple met her eyes everywhere she turned. "Is it always like this?" she breathed.

Hattie's face reflected the glory of the sunset. "Almost always," she said softly. "It's times like these when I feel closest to God. I love the sunsets here."

Most people were not so open in speaking about God. Jenny felt slightly uncomfortable, but watching Hattie's face she once again felt a yearning to have that same sense of joy. She had never met anyone quite like Hattie. Her faith was as real and natural as the woman herself.

Jenny's father and mother had always had a deep faith that they had tried to pass on to their offspring. Somehow she had gotten away from that in college and it hadn't occurred to her that perhaps that was something her brother and sister needed right now. Guilt clogged her throat as she realized that she had failed her parents in this regard.

It was late when they reached Hattie's home, a low, sprawling building with immaculate desert landscaping. The twins came out to meet them with Mark following at a leisurely pace. Being fourteen, Mark felt the need to maintain some superiority, although the grin he gave his mother was endearingly boyish.

"Hi," he drawled. "The kids and I had pizza for supper. That okay?"

Although Renee ignored him, David obviously couldn't let the matter of being called a kid slide by without some comment. "If we're kids, what's that make you?"

"Why, I'm the kid sitter," he stated, his eyes twinkling with a humor he had obviously inherited from his mother.

David punched him good-humoredly on the arm. It was obvious that David and Mark had become fast friends despite the difference in their ages. Renee, on the other hand, held herself aloof, but Jenny watched her quick glances at Mark when she thought no one was looking. He was certainly a handsome lad, Jenny mused, with an athletic build and dark auburn hair. If he was anything like his mother he would undoubtedly be good for David.

Hattie and Jenny finished off the remaining pizza and lounged back in their chairs. "A hot bath would be heavenly right about now," Hattie moaned.

Jenny sat up quickly. "Oh, my goodness! I forgot about the bathroom! We can't use the bathtub yet." She slid back down in her chair dejectedly. "That means we need to clean the bathroom before we can go to bed."

Hattie handed Jenny the keys to an old car of her husband's that she had told Jenny he no longer used and she was welcome to borrow. Brown eyes regarded her sympathetically. "Why don't you stay the night here and go back to the ranch tomorrow?"

"I couldn't put you to all that trouble. I appreciate all you've done for us already, but I can't continue to impose on your hospitality."

Jenny rose slowly from her chair, stiffness at the unaccustomed exercise already telling on her muscles.

"It's no trouble, really."

"Aw, Jen," David whined. "Can't we stay? I don't want to go back to that old musty cabin tonight."

Renee said nothing, but Jenny noticed the tired droop of her shoulders. She was being so sweet about all of this upheaval in their lives. It suddenly became too much. Jenny's body sagged and, turning to Hattie, she gave a tremulous smile. "Thanks. We'd like to stay, if you're sure it's no trouble."

Hattie breathed an obvious sigh of relief. "Of course you won't be any trouble. Jacob won't be home until tomorrow night, anyway. His business in Prescott took longer than he anticipated. Besides, we have plenty of room."

The room Hattie took them to was a beautiful blend of the colors Jenny had just witnessed in the sunset. The walls were a pale melon color and the comforter on the bed was a mixture of pale sand, green and soft peach in a Native geometric pattern. Brown Saltillo floor tiles peeped from beneath a large area rug, also finished in a Native design. "This room is lovely," Jenny told her.

From the other side of the room Renee was running her hand gently over an antique dresser. "Mother would have loved this room," she stated quietly. Tears were very near the surface and to help stave them off Jenny pasted a smile on her own tired face.

"Come on, love. You're tired. Let's get you ready for bed."

When the kids were safely in bed, Jenny sat across from Hattie, who was sitting on the sofa in the living room. Her gaze wandered slowly around, taking in the quiet, under-stated elegance of the furnishings. Hattie Ames had ex-cellent taste in decorating. It was obvious that the Ameses were wealthy people, yet they didn't flaunt it.

"Can I get you something?" Hattie's soft voice broke into Jenny's reflections. "Would you like a drink? Coffee? Tea?"

Jenny shook her head. "Thank you, no. I was just ad-miring your home. It's beautiful."

"Thank you." She smiled mischievously. "Realty is ac-tually a hobby with me. My real love is taking care of my family."

"Have you any other children besides Mark?"

"Oh, yes. Our daughter April is the oldest. She goes to the University of Northern Arizona. Normally she comes home for the summer, but this year she and her roommate decided to stay to see if they could complete a few sum-mer courses." She picked up a picture from the table behind her and handed it to Jenny. "Paul is my middle child. He's sixteen and has volunteered as a counselor at our church's Bible camp for the summer."

Jenny studied the photo. A laughing Hattie was sur-rounded by a tall, good-looking man in his mid-forties who was looking at her as though she was the most beau-tiful woman in the world. A dark-haired pixie of a girl was curled gracefully at her feet and two boys almost identical in appearance leaned in from each side. She recognized Mark; his brother was an older replica.

Hattie got to her feet, stifling a yawn. "I'm for bed. How about you?"

Jenny also rose slowly to her feet. Her back still ached, her knees were sore and she felt decidedly out of place. Almost like a ship tossing in the wind. But tomorrow, Jenny reflected, tomorrow was the beginning of a new life.

As she showered and prepared for bed her thoughts drifted to the events of the day. The cabin would take a lot of cleaning and there were some repairs that needed to be made, but all in all it would be a wonderful home. As she had told David, paradise compared with what they had had to live in for the past few years. She wondered if they had other neighbors besides Mitch Anderson.

She crawled between the cool sheets and tried to free her mind from its confusing thoughts, but little worries kept coming back to plague her. There was so much she needed to accomplish and she was unsure of where to start. Thankfully, she had a wonderful friend in Hattie Ames. But what of Mitch? She wondered exactly what unknown component he would bring to her life. What had he thought of her, anyway? She smiled to herself in the dark. Her last waking reflection was that he probably hadn't given her a thought one way or the other.

Jenny would have been surprised to know that at that very moment Mitch was standing on the veranda of his ranch house trying to dispel memories of Jenny that had frequented his thoughts all day. He was disappointed, to say the least. Mitch wanted Tito's property to help expand his business enterprises, hoping to embark upon a new venture that was more for pleasure than for profit.

A girl alone with two kids. Mitch shook his head in aggravation at her stubborn refusal to listen to reason. He could still see incredibly long lashes curled over flashing sapphire eyes. Staring into those eyes, he had felt as though she'd extracted a portion of his soul, inspected it and found it lacking. A feeling that was decidedly unsettling and not something he cared to repeat. Her eyes had taken on a strange glow fueled by her anger, but he had sensed that she'd felt the connection, as well, and had been just as disturbed by it.

She was certainly nothing to look at, except for those tantalizing eyes, but he had to give her credit for her grit. Now the question was how much stamina did she have? Besides all the other problems he could think of, Tito's cabin had no air-conditioning and the temperatures were soaring.

If his mother and ex-fiancée were anything to go by, he didn't foresee a long stay. A wicked grin sliced across his face. Wait until she experienced her first rattlesnake, scorpion or dust storm. He'd give her the benefit of the doubt. She'd probably last a month. Maybe.

For some reason the thought of her leaving didn't give him the thrill he expected. Aggravated with himself, he turned and went inside.

Chapter 3

Jenny leaned her palms against the porch rails and stared out over the sandy desert that surrounded her. The sun was sinking slowly in the west and casting fingers of vermilion and purple across the sky. Already the hot temperatures of the day were beginning to cool.

A feeling of euphoria enveloped her. If she lived to be a hundred years old she would never cease to marvel at the beauty of these sunsets. She could well understand Hattie's statement about feeling closer to God at times such as these.

Thinking back over the day's events, she was more than satisfied with what she had accomplished. Thankfully, Hattie had invited Renee and David to stay with her while Jenny returned to the cabin to finish cleaning. Maybe she should have insisted on their help, but she still felt guilty insisting that they live here. Perhaps when she finished with the cabin, they would be more amenable and see what she saw in this desolate but awe-inspiring place.

A soft smile curved her lips. David had actually begged

to be allowed to spend the night with Mark so that he could attend church with him in the morning. Her David. Already she could see the advantages of living here. Even Renee was showing signs of benefitting from the changed environment. Although still unusually glum, Jenny could sense a release of anxiety in Renee's attitude. And Hattie's genuine faith made Jenny want to be back among people who loved the Lord, to once again have that feeling of family.

As the last rays of sunlight slowly disappeared over the horizon, darkness crept over the land. Turning, she went back into the cabin, flicking the switch beside the front door. She looked around and felt a surge of pride in what she had achieved. All the rooms were freshly cleaned and a faint scent of pine permeated the air. There was no longer the feeling of neglect she had experienced when she'd first arrived. The cabin seemed to warmly embrace her in her solitude. She didn't feel lonely, only contented.

She walked into the kitchen and went to the refrigerator. Opening it, she peered in and pulled out the meal she had fixed for herself earlier. Just because she was on her own didn't mean she had to forgo having a civilized meal.

She set a crisp salad on the table, following it with a cold ham, turkey and roast beef sandwich. The sweltering summer heat made the cold food a welcome respite after hours of intense, sweaty exercise. A juicy nectarine would do for dessert, she decided, marveling at the change in her appetite. She was thankful, because, as Hattie had pointed out, she could definitely use a few pounds.

Remembering the long inspection Mitch Anderson had given her brought hot color flooding to her face. His look had been anything but complimentary. She snorted in frustration at having the man constantly jumping into her thoughts with the least provocation, and firmly pushed him from her mind.

Laying the silverware beside her place setting she experienced a moment's guilt over her contentment without her brother and sister. It had been so long since she had been able to have time to herself and she was thoroughly enjoying this respite from burdens and responsibilities. She loved David and Renee, but being a single parent of teenagers when she herself was only twenty-six was taxing.

She had given up so much, basically her whole life, and yet she rarely experienced any feelings of regret. But there were times when she wished life could be different. Not only for herself but for David and Renee, also. She felt ill-equipped to handle the mounting pressures being foisted upon her by young adolescents.

Jenny seated herself at the table and laid her napkin on her lap. She refused to spend the remaining free hours in the doldrums or feeling guilty.

The rest of the evening she wandered from room to room planning redecorating schemes. If she wanted television reception, she would have to get a satellite dish since cable service wasn't available this far out. Just another thing to add to the mounting costs of living here.

Only one thing still made her uncomfortable. Every time she went into the bathroom she was assaulted by the presence of the broken pane of glass. The cabin was situated so far out in the desert, she wondered if it could have truly been vandals or something much more sinister.

Sitting on the sofa, contemplating the problem, she suddenly heard an eerie, keening howl penetrate the darkness outside. She sat frozen, her face blanching. What seemed an interminable length of time later a second howl answered the first.

The howling grew louder and seemed to be coming closer. Chills ran up and down her spine like a herd of galloping horses. She shivered and pulled her knees up under her chin. Maybe it hadn't been such a good idea to stay here alone, after all, especially since she'd forgotten to have the phone turned back on. Chastising herself for her lack of courage, she reminded herself that at least she was safe here in the cabin with the door and windows shut.

Remembering the broken pane of glass in the bathroom, her overactive imagination suddenly went on a rampage. She had heard that wolves could scent their prey from great distances. If so, could they smell her through that small hole and would they lunge through the bathroom window trying to get to her, as they did in the movies? The image of a wolf crashing through the glass, teeth bared, made her heart triple its already pounding rhythm.

Jumping up, she ran to the bathroom to close the door. At least if they got into the bathroom, there would be a solid barrier between her and them, but then what? Her normally sensible mind refused to function properly as the howls continued to sound ever closer.

As she reached out for the knob to the bathroom door, something fell onto her outstretched hand and then onto the floor. Her eyes widened in alarm when she recognized the insect with the curled tail and pincers. Nerves already taut from terror, she jerked backward and screamed.

A sudden pounding on her door only increased her hysteria. The wolves were trying to break down the door! She ran for the fireplace and grabbed the fireplace iron from its rack just as the front door slammed back against the wall. She clutched her throat, panic paralyzing her vocal chords.

"What is going on in here?"

Mitch stood in the doorway of the cabin, his hands curled into fists and his pulse pounding with the speed of a runaway train. His eyes swiftly circled the room and came to rest on Jenny huddled in the corner clutching a fireplace iron as if her life depended on it. Recognition registered in her eyes a moment before her legs buckled under her and she slowly slid to the floor.

Mitch was at her side in an instant. Kneeling beside her, he placed a protective arm around her as he continued to survey the room for the threat that had turned her into a quivering bundle of nerves. His heart was thrumming in rhythm with the pulse he could see jerking in her throat. Seeing no immediate threat, he frowned.

He lifted her to her feet and searched for injuries. "What's happened? Are you hurt?"

At her shuddering sighs, he pried the fireplace iron from her tightly fisted hands and laid it aside. She was shaking like a leaf in a hurricane. He wrapped her comfortingly in his arms and started crooning soft words of reassurance as he took in the fact that there was no visible danger. One large hand held her head gently against his chest, his other hand slowly stroked her back. He wasn't sure if his shirt would ever be the same after the mangling it was receiving from her clenching hands. He could feel the tension slowly leave her body as she relaxed against him. Her trembling lessened and her tears finally ceased.

"Can you tell me what happened?" he asked softly after she was silent for several seconds. She visibly tried to pull herself together.

The sudden realization that she was in his arms seemed to register and she pushed back, folding her arms across her chest defensively. When she could finally bring herself to look him in the face, traces of tears still lingered on her lashes.

"Wolves!" she choked out, begging him with her eyes to believe her.

"What?" Mitch watched her, a frown tugging his brows together. What was she talking about? There were no wolves in this part of the state.

"Didn't you hear them? Didn't you see them outside?" Her voice rose in panic on the last word. Mitch's eyes narrowed speculatively as he considered whether the woman just might be slightly unbalanced.

Trying to calm her again, he reached forward and took her by the shoulders. She was still shaking and he felt every protective instinct he thought he had buried years ago rise to the surface again.

"We don't have wolves around here," he told her quietly.

Pushing his hands away, she glared at him. "But I heard them. Just now."

Sudden comprehension lit his features and he chuckled in relief. "Those weren't wolves you heard. They were coyotes."

"Coyotes?"

He nodded, watching her carefully for any returning signs of hysteria. Instead hot color stole into her cheeks.

"Oh. I hadn't thought of that. We had coyotes in North Dakota, too."

Mitch hid a grin. Maybe he was wrong. Maybe she wouldn't last a month, after all.

A new thought darkened her eyes and she whirled toward the bathroom. She glanced frantically around the living room. "There was a scorpion, too."

Mitch frowned. "Where?"

"In the bathroom. No, I mean it came from the bathroom. It fell on my arm!"

He could tell she was struggling not to panic again in front of him. He took her by the arms. "Did it sting you?" he asked anxiously as he inspected her skin for injury. Although people rarely died from scorpion stings, they could be extremely painful.

She shook her head, biting her bottom lip as she tried to pull from his hold. Soft skin covered the slightest set of bones he had ever seen. He was almost afraid of crushing her with his big hands. He opened his mouth to reassure her when he caught movement from the corner of his eye. He held out his hand. "Hand me the fireplace iron."

Without hesitation, Jenny hastily held it out to him. Surprised that he was reluctant to release her, he took the iron and, using it as a hammer, swiftly killed the offending insect and scooped it up with the end. Walking to the door, he quickly dispatched the creature outside. When he turned back to the room he tried hard to stifle the grin that was trying to push its way through.

"Anything else?" One blond brow quirked upward as he held out the fireplace iron to her, his lips still twitching.

She flushed with embarrassment. Taking the iron, she walked across the room and slammed it back into the rack. "You needn't act so superior."

He couldn't help the grin then, but he refrained from comment. Now that the drama was finished, he could finally breathe. His heart was only now resuming its normal rhythm. Hearing Jenny's scream had sent adrenaline rushing through him in a torrent. Holding her in his arms hadn't helped much, either. It was going to be some time before those lingering memories would fade. Even now, the soft scent of jasmine remained in his mind.

He slowly wandered around the cabin, noting the changes she had made. He raked his hands through his hair, sighed and glanced her way. "You're really going through with it. You're really going to stay here."

He saw her tense.

"What are you doing here, anyway?" She contemplated him through narrowed eyes. "If you came to talk me out of my ranch, you can just leave again."

When he took a step toward her she hastily removed herself to the other side of the room, placing the sofa between them. She glared at him warily and his aggravation mounted.

"Look, I don't know what you have against me, but I'm not the big, bad ogre you make me out to be."

At her cynical look, he sighed. "All right. Maybe I haven't been exactly welcoming."

She gave a very unladylike snort, but said nothing.

Okay, so he hadn't been the friendliest person she would ever meet, but she didn't have to look at him as though he was a dragon about to devour her, either. He forced himself to relax.

"I came to let you know that you have a horse at my ranch. It actually belonged to Tito, but I've been keeping him until someone came to claim the estate."

"A horse? Mine? I mean, ours?" A glow of pleasure lit her eyes. When she smiled that way, her sapphire eyes sparkled with an inner fire that made her almost pretty despite her wraithlike figure. He remembered the feel of those bones beneath his hands, so frail, so small. He pushed such thoughts aside, aggravated with himself for allowing her to get under his skin that way and make him feel protective toward her.

"What kind of horse is it?"

"He's a gelded quarter horse." How much did she know about caring for a horse? He had been reluctant to even mention it to her, wondering if the horse would suffer under her care. That was something he wasn't willing to let happen. The horse had been a favorite of Tito's.

"I'm willing to buy him from you."

The pleasure died in her eyes. "Is that all you ever think about? Buying, buying, buying! I've known men like you. You think money can buy you anything!"

They both stood frozen for an interminable second before Jenny clapped a hand over her mouth, her eyes widening in horror. "I'm sorry!"

But it was too late; his temper flared into life. He was across the room in three strides, stepping up and over the couch she had assumed would be a barrier against him. She flinched away from him, backing until she was against the wall. He placed two corded arms at each side of her head and leaned his face close to hers. Anger blazed from his eyes.

"Listen, Jenny Gordon, I'm getting a little tired of your judgmental attitude. I was thinking of the horse when I made the offer. I didn't know if you knew how to care for a horse or even if you had the money to." At the mention of money Jenny winced. "Ah, I can see you didn't think of that. Well, Miss Gordon, I did. Horses need a lot of care and attention, and they cost money. I didn't want to see the horse come to grief because you couldn't handle the obligation."

Jenny stared into his green eyes, appalled and embarrassed at her outburst. Something about Mitch always put her on the defensive. Just for a moment, her imagination had morphed his face into a picture of Alexander's, bringing back all the hurt she had thought finally laid to rest. She'd struck out at Mitch, the only available target around.

Why did she continually suspect Mitch of ulterior motives? Despite his kindness tonight, she was still wary of him. Maybe it had to do with her unusual physical reaction to him, or maybe it had to do with those hateful memories from her past. Whenever he came near, her heart doubled its rhythm and her knees weakened, something that had never happened to her before, even with Alexander. If Alexander had been dangerous, this man was positively lethal. Just being around him fired up every one of her self-protective instincts.

She sighed. "I'm truly sorry. You're right. I'm not equipped to deal with the finances of maintaining a horse right now." She pulled her gaze from his and dropped it to the floor. "It's just that I wanted it so badly. It would be wonderful for my brother and sister. It's been a long time since they've been able to have a pet."

Mitch pushed himself away from the wall and stood towering over her. He stared for a long time, his face clouded with uncertainty. Then heaving a deep sigh, he said, "I think we got off on the wrong foot. Can we just start over?"

She couldn't breathe until he moved away and gave her some room. Nodding her head, she told him in a voice that was a little too breathy for comfort, "I'd like that."

She motioned for him to have a seat and he moved to the sofa and lowered himself onto it. Jenny settled guardedly on a chair opposite him.

He was staring at her in that way that made her feel self-conscious. What did he see when he looked at her? She knew that she was no beauty queen, but it was something she hadn't given much thought to in quite some time.

Raising two kids on her own with few resources hadn't left much time to worry about something as inconsequential as her looks. It bothered her that it suddenly seemed so important now. When the silence became uncomfortable, she opened her mouth to offer him a drink, but he interrupted her.

"Jenny?" He paused. "May I call you that?" She nodded and he continued, "I happen to know that Tito didn't leave much money with his estate." He watched her carefully. "Just how do you plan to live out here?"

She was prepared for the question, but not with the answer. It was something she had been struggling with for days. Shrugging her shoulders, she looked down at her hands folded in her lap. "I'm not sure." She hesitated before looking him fully in the face. "If I'm careful with the little money I get from the estate, I figure we can manage several months. By then I hope to have a job."

Mitch slowly shook his head. "This is a very small town and there aren't a lot of jobs. Your only chance would be to find work someplace else. Maybe Dewey or Prescott. Maybe even Phoenix since jobs are pretty scarce even in Dewey and Prescott."

"Well, I'm sure I can find something. I'm not picky."

He was already shaking his head again. "You still don't get it, do you? Dewey is about thirty miles from this cabin and Prescott a good twenty more than that. Phoenix is around ninety."

Jenny gulped. With the cost of gas, commuting to such

jobs would certainly cut down on any income she could hope to receive.

"I'll find something," she insisted stubbornly.

Mitch leaned back on the sofa, languidly crossing one leg over the other. His indolence didn't fool her for a second. He was obviously thinking something, and thinking hard from the looks of him. But whatever it was, he was keeping it to himself.

"I'll keep the gelding for the time being. Let me know when you want him back. Will you promise me one thing?" he asked.

Jenny eyed him suspiciously.

"What?" she asked warily.

He leaned forward, folding his hands and draping them between his legs. "When—I mean, *if* you decide to sell this place, I'd like you to let me know first. Would you do that?"

Surely that wasn't so much to ask, she thought. She wasn't sure just why Mitch wanted the land so much, but if she decided to sell, it might just as well be to him.

"I'll keep that in mind," she told him finally. "Tell me about the horse. What's his name? How old is he?"

Mitch's lips quirked at the corners at her obvious attempt to derail him from further arguments. Following her lead, they talked for several hours about trivial things, without either one giving away much personal information.

A sudden hush settled on the room, neither one able to think of anything to say for the moment. As the silence lengthened, Jenny became increasingly nervous. Glancing up she caught Mitch watching her intently. She quickly glanced away.

Clearing her throat, she was about to make some inane comment when she heard a familiar wailing from outside. Her eyes widened in alarm, flying back to mesh with his laughing ones. Knowing he was amused she tried to stop her body from reacting, but a shiver shook through her at the eerie sound.

A small smile played at his lips. "Funny thing about coyotes. They're more afraid of people than people are of them."

Jenny knew that, but being here alone with her overactive imagination had definitely disconcerted her. When she'd heard coyotes at the farm she had always been surrounded by family, which had given her a feeling of security.

"It's nature, Jenny."

The soft caressing way he said her name caused her to shiver in a much different way. What was it about him that was so compellingly attractive? It wasn't just his looks. He exuded a presence that made her feel incredibly safe. He was what could be called a macho male and the feminine woman in her responded to it.

He glanced at his watch and rose languidly to his feet. For being such a big man, he moved with catlike grace.

"I need to go."

Jenny rose and walked with him to the door. Opening it, he turned and leaned against the frame. "The scorpions will always be here. You just have to learn to live with them. It's part of life here, like coyotes. Nature is pretty untamed here. You adjust."

She watched him carefully. The simplicity of his words was belied by the intensity of his voice. Was he trying to be helpful or merely frighten her? She didn't know, but she was grateful that he had come when he had.

"Thanks." She smiled up at him. It was all she could think of to say and encompassed everything she was trying *not* to say.

He grinned back in understanding. "Glad to help."

Turning, he walked across the porch and down the steps. Jenny noticed his Jeep parked in front of the house. A rueful smile curled her lips. He had arrived and she hadn't even been aware, so frightened was she at the time. Now, although she was still a little nervous about the coyotes, and though the scorpions still sent shivers down her spine, she wasn't afraid anymore. Mitch curled himself into the vehicle, barely glancing her way before he put it into gear and turned back toward the road.

Jenny watched until his taillights were a mere speck in the distance before she went inside. She walked into the bathroom gingerly, glancing nervously around. Taking an old towel, she stuffed it into the broken pane.

"There," she told herself aloud, "maybe that will keep those critters out." She laughed somewhat nervously. It was time for bed, but not before she had a bath. She peeked carefully into the tub and sighed with relief at its emptiness. Turning on the taps, she went to get her pajamas.

It was well past midnight, she marveled. She hadn't realized it was so late. Where had the time gone? Mitch could be an amusing companion when he chose to be. Which was the real Mitch, the surly man who made her feel less than human, or the charming man who made her feel safe and secure? Regardless, she needed to push him from her mind. He was too attractive and she, she was beginning to realize, was not as immune to his charms as she should be.

Chapter 4

Settling into a routine at the cabin was much easier than Jenny had anticipated. Much of this was due to David's being able to spend a lot of time with Mark. Having a friend, even one older than himself, had been good for David.

Someone else who seemed to be having a big impact on David's life was Mitch Anderson. It was the beginning of August and in the three weeks they had lived here David had never missed a church service. He not only wanted to go on Sundays, but on Wednesday nights, as well. David had a bad case of what amounted to hero worship.

Jenny couldn't fault him for it, since she realized that Mitch truly enjoyed kids. Hattie had told her that since Mitch had taken over the junior high boy's class, the boys had left much of their adolescent behavior behind and were beginning to mature spiritually.

Jenny questioned how spiritually mature Mitch might be, but since that would be akin to the pot calling the kettle black, she refrained from voicing her doubts.

As for Renee, since they'd been attending church a new softness had entered her demeanor. She was more spiritually inclined although she seemed to have an obsession with the afterlife. Her constant questions were beginning to bother Jenny, especially since she knew she was not equipped to deal with the answers.

Something that bothered Jenny more was the fact that she still had no source of income. Her savings was almost exhausted and she had not been able to accomplish as much as she had wanted with cabin repairs and renovations. Jacob had promised her that she should be receiving the money from Cousin Tito's estate early the next week so she wasn't as concerned as she might have been, but what was she going to do when that money ran out?

Mitch had been right. She couldn't find a job in Mayer or in Dewey and she hesitated to look even further in Prescott. She had a little time, but time had a way of getting away from you.

Their few household goods arrived much later than expected so they'd had to make do with what they had brought for nearly two weeks. Still, their shipment finally came and it was good to be surrounded by familiar things.

Sighing gently, she continued kneading the dough for the bread she was making. It had never occurred to her at the time she'd taken home economics courses at the University of North Dakota that they would be so useful to her. She had loved home ec, and had decided that perhaps she might like to teach the course when she graduated. Mother had called her a regular little homebody.

Jenny smiled. At least she could cook and she was aching to decorate the cabin and make it homier. Problems aside, she had thoroughly enjoyed herself the past few weeks. Life was good, she decided.

David came through the door, perspiration dripping from his face. Wiping it away with the front of his shirt, he moaned, "Man, it's hot out there! Do you know what the temperature is?"

Jenny shook her head. "No, I haven't had time to turn on the radio."

He left the kitchen and returned in moments with the radio. Plugging it into the outlet above the counter, he fiddled with the dials until he found a Phoenix radio station.

"There are some dark clouds building up farther north," he told her. "Looks like we might get some rain."

Jenny's first experience with the Arizona monsoon season had been impressive, to say the least. It still boggled her mind that a desert could have a monsoon. Weren't monsoons supposed to be wet and steamy and limited to tropical countries? Although there had been many dark, billowy clouds, they had yet to receive any rain. Only what the locals called dust storms; blowing dust, black clouds and severe winds.

Wiping the perspiration from her face with a paper towel she wondered for the hundredth time why Cousin Tito hadn't installed air-conditioning. He must have had the constitution of an ox. Each day temperatures had soared to the high nineties, cooling somewhat at night. It surprised her that an area that could be so hot in the day could turn so cool at night.

Renee walked into the kitchen and plopped down on one of the hefty wooden kitchen chairs. She had folded a piece of paper and was fanning herself with it.

"When do you think we'll be able to get some real fans?" she asked.

Jenny sat across from her and handed her a glass of iced tea, placing her own on the table in front of her.

"I don't know. We have to wait to see how much the settlement is after lawyer's fees and such." She twirled her glass, sliding a finger over the moist rivulets of condensation dripping down the sides.

David came and sat at the table with them. "I wish I

could go to Mark's," he complained. "At least he has a pool."

"Well, for that matter, he has air-conditioning, too," Renee told him drily. "But what good does that do us? We can't live with the Ameses, for crying out loud."

Both David and Jenny stared at her speechless. This was the first time in a long while that Renee had reverted to the irascible kid she'd once been. Jenny smiled to herself but David found nothing to be amused at.

"Who said anything about living with them? Can't a guy say anything around here without someone jumping on him?"

"If I were jumping on you," Renee retorted, "you'd know about it."

"Enough," Jenny told them.

Renee picked up her tea but David slid down in his chair, a sulky expression on his face.

The announcer on the radio interrupted the regular programming to give a weather report. A flash-flood watch had been issued for Yavapai, Maricopa and Coconino counties.

"Well," David told them, getting up from his seat and going to the window, "that includes us. Looks like we're going to get some rain, after all."

"How do you know that?" Jenny asked.

He threw her an impatient look. "Mitch told us in Bible class."

Jenny frowned. "In Bible class? What do the Arizona counties have to do with the Bible?" Shouldn't he be teaching the Bible in Bible class? What was Mitch teaching them, anyway? she wondered.

"Mitch was comparing the Israeli provinces with counties in Arizona. I just happen to remember that he told us we were in Yavapai County."

"Oh." Jenny felt slightly ashamed that she had once again judged the man unfairly. What on earth was there about him that made her want to see only the worst in him? She had only to hear his name and she immediately jumped to erroneous conclusions.

"It sure is getting dark," Renee interjected, joining her brother at the window.

Jenny went out onto the front porch, David and Renee following close behind. The sky to the northeast was churning with billowy dark clouds. Huge, white, anvil-shaped clouds swelled upward in the center, thousands of feet into the air. Periodically, flashes of light could be seen illuminating them from within. Such a sight was truly awe-inspiring.

In North Dakota there had been routine tornadoes, but David and Renee were too young to remember them well. Not even the swirling sky, tinted with green that Jenny knew to be tornado weather, was as magnificent as the huge formation of clouds that seemed to surround them now.

"I'm scared, Jen."

Jenny could see that Renee was truly frightened. She placed an arm around her shoulders and felt her trembling.

"Let's go back inside and look at that pattern book again to see if we can't choose something to make for your first day in school."

Flashes of light were followed by heavy rumbling in the distance. David glanced around him, swallowing hard. "I think I'll see if I can help." He looked around at Renee. "After all, I don't want you to look frumpy and embarrass me."

Jenny pinched Renee's shoulder lightly when she would have answered him. David was trying so hard to be a man, but there were times when the little boy in him would come out. It wasn't easy trying to be the man of the house when you were twelve years old.

"Good idea, David," Jenny agreed, "and maybe Renee can help you, too."

"Yeah, right. I already know what I want," he told them.

Gathering on the sofa, a twin on each side of her, Jenny pulled out the pattern book. Sewing was just another useful thing she had learned in college, she thought wryly. She could cook, clean, sew and a host of other such things, and yet she had no skills that would help her to get a job. How could that be?

David flipped through the book until he came across a page of Western wear. "That," he said, pointing to a Western shirt and jeans. "Can I get a Stetson, too," he asked Jenny, "and some cowboy boots?"

Renee groaned. "Who's going to be embarrassed by whom?"

"What's wrong with dressing Western," he snapped. "It's what everybody wears around here."

Before Jenny could intervene the air was split by a flash of light so brilliant it was nearly blinding to the eyes. They all flinched and jumped when it was followed by a loud, crackling boom of thunder that literally shook the cabin. A torrent of rain suddenly pounded the roof, cascading off the edges in rivulets. The wind intensified, rattling the panes of glass. Renee's eyes widened in alarm and not for the first time Jenny wished heartily that there were curtains at the windows so that she could block out the fearsome sight.

David flipped hastily through the pages. "Let's see, Renee." His voice trembled slightly. "I think you'd look good in this."

Reluctantly averting her eyes from the window, Renee glanced at the dress he was pointing to. Forgetting the storm, her eyebrows pulled together in a frown. "Are you crazy? I wouldn't be caught dead in that!"

For the next hour all three playfully argued over clothes, trying their best to ignore the raging storm outside. Even in North Dakota they had never experienced anything of this magnitude.

Before long the rain stopped and the thunder was once

again reduced to a mere rumble in the distance. Jenny pushed the book aside.

"You guys decide what you want and let me know," she told them. "Right now I have to get my potato rolls in the oven."

Later that evening when the twins were in bed, Jenny found her favorite spot on the porch and leaned her arms against the rails. The air smelled fresh and clean after the storm. The temperature had cooled dramatically and Jenny was thankful for the relief from the intense heat. She could still see flashes of lightning off to the southwest. The stars were hidden from view by the dark clouds milling across the night sky.

As she thought over the past weeks, a small spark of hope stirred within her. Renee was beginning to return to normal and David no longer seemed to pine for his friends in New York. Looking up at the night sky she prayed for the first time in a very long time. Her prayer was a simple one. *Thank You, Lord.*

The next day Jenny was shaking the rug from her bedroom over the porch rails when she spotted a vehicle approaching. She felt a sudden lurch in her stomach until she recognized Hattie's car and not a blue Jeep. She smiled, laying the rug across the rails and tripping lightly down the steps. When the car stopped she saw that Hattie was a passenger and her husband, Jacob, the driver.

The car had barely ceased its motion before Hattie threw open the passenger door and flung herself out of the car. There wasn't a slow bone in Hattie's body. She was like a live wire full of energy.

"Hi!" She was practically chirruping. "Have we got some good news for you!"

Jacob was more dignified in his exit from the car, pulling his briefcase out behind him. Even in the extreme heat, he looked immaculate in his three-piece suit. He smiled ruefully at Jenny and shook his head. "Never let it be said that my Hattie can't keep a secret." He grinned fondly at his wife.

"Oh, you." Hattie punched him lightly on his arm. "I didn't say a thing."

Jenny and Jacob exchanged amused glances. Jacob only shook his head again.

"So come in," Jenny told them, "and tell me the good news."

When they were seated in the living room, Jacob laid his briefcase on the coffee table. Flipping it open, he extracted some papers, riffling through them briefly.

"I need you to sign a few papers," he told her, handing her the papers and his gold pen. "Take your time and look them over before signing."

"We couldn't reach you by phone," Hattie told her, "since you don't have one yet. And since Jacob thought it couldn't wait, I decided to come along and keep him company."

Jacob grinned. "In other words, she wanted the scoop before anyone else."

Throwing him a look of reproach, Hattie told Jenny, "If my husband wasn't so closemouthed about his clients, I wouldn't have to be so devious."

Jenny took a moment to read the documents and then scrawled her signature across the bottom of the indicated papers. After taking the documents back, Jacob handed her a slip of paper. Realizing it was a cashier's check, color suffused her face and a sparkle came to her eyes. The amount was more than she had expected. She smiled broadly at them. "Thank you so much! You don't know how much this means to me. I wasn't expecting it until next week."

Jacob smiled. "I thought you might like to have it now, and since I wasn't working in Prescott today I decided I'd bring it to you." He glanced over at his wife. "Or should I say, I thought *we'd* bring it to you."

Hattie reached across the table and squeezed Jenny's

hand. "I'm glad you could have the money early," she said. "I know how much you've been counting on it. Now you can do some of the things you wanted to do to the cabin."

"Not too much," Jenny told her. "I don't know how long this money is going to have to last." Wrinkling her nose, she told them, "But one of the first things I'm going to do is replace that window in the bathroom."

Hattie gazed around her. "You've certainly made a difference in this place. Tito was not the neatest person in the world, but at least he kept the place decent. You, however, have added the feminine touches that make a house a home."

"Can I get you something to drink?" Jenny asked them, but Jacob was already shaking his head.

"No, thanks. We have to pick Paul up at camp."

Jenny walked them to the door when something seemed to occur to Hattie. "Where are Renee and David?"

When she told them that Mitch Anderson had picked up the twins and taken them to his place to ride Dynamo, their gelding, Hattie looked surprised. "Why didn't you go, too?"

"I had work to do," Jenny told her, refusing to be drawn into a discussion about her conflicting feelings where Mitch was concerned. The sly look on Hattie's face told Jenny she hadn't been fooled. The cabin was immaculate and she had no job, so what work could be so pressing that she couldn't have gone with the twins?

At Hattie's dubious look Jenny hastily turned toward Jacob. "Thank you again for bringing the check. I guess I'll go pick up the twins and head for town and deposit it. I think maybe a little shopping might be good for all of us. Maybe we'll even go to Prescott and have a look around."

A few minutes later Jenny watched their departing car disappear down the road. Shaking her head, she went back inside, retreating from her thoughts. Maybe she would change clothes before she picked up the twins. She hadn't dressed up in a long time. It was only because she wanted to celebrate, she assured herself. If there was another reason, she refused to admit it even to herself.

An hour later Jenny pulled into Mitch's driveway and stared in wonder around her. Even though she'd seen Mitch's place before, she was still awed by it. Mitch had created a small oasis in the middle of the desert. How had he done it? A low, sprawling ranch house sat in the middle of a lush green circle of grass surrounded by multicolored rocks formed into a rectangle, which in turn gradually blended into the desert terrain around it. Palm trees swayed majestically as a backdrop and large paloverdes offered shade. A veranda surrounded the house on three sides. Deck furniture nestled against the walls. Corral fencing wound its way along the drive and the property line, adding just the right touch of rustic simplicity.

A much smaller version of Mitch's stables and a similar corral structure sat behind Jenny's cabin. Jenny assumed the corral at her house was for Dynamo.

Sliding out of the car, she stood, hesitating, trying to decide whether to go to the house or to the stables. Her decision was made for her when she heard a yell from the direction of the stables.

"Jen! Come see!"

David's head had appeared around the door of the building, a huge grin splitting his face. Waving frantically, he motioned for her to come that way.

Walking across, she noticed other things she had missed before. She could see behind the house now and saw that Mitch had a pool surrounded by a redwood deck. Patio furniture glistened in the sun. A helicopter sitting on a pad took up a large area off to her right. What an awful lot of money it must take to keep this place in such perfect condition. The indications of Mitch's wealth made her suddenly uneasy.

When she reached David, he grabbed her hand and pulled her inside.

"Mitch thought he heard a car. He told me to check to see who it was." He stopped suddenly and looked her over slowly. "Gosh, Jen. What have you done to yourself?"

Glancing up she noticed Mitch was coming, his long legs eating up the distance between them. The sudden cart-wheels in her stomach brought a frown to her face. She still hadn't yet decided if she liked him, but he definitely caused a reaction. She fervently hoped he hadn't heard David's exclamation because she didn't want him to think she had dressed up and put on makeup to impress him.

"Welcome to the Double A," he told her as his eyes drifted slowly over her. If he noticed anything out of the ordinary he gave no sign. "I would have returned the twins. You didn't have to come all this way."

Jenny could feel the flush warming her cheeks. "I decided to do some shopping in Prescott, and I thought I'd take the twins with me."

Renee hurtled herself forward, stopping breathless in front of Jenny. "Oh, Jen. You've got to see him again!" she enthused. "He's absolutely gorgeous."

Smiling, Jenny followed Renee to a stall in the corner. Even Mitch's stables were in excellent condition.

She caught her breath when she saw the gelding. He was, as Renee had suggested, gorgeous. Sleek and shiny, Dynamo's brown coat gleamed with vitality. Huge, soulful brown eyes stared at her. Reaching out a hand, she slowly caressed his neck. Their old farm horse had been nothing like this.

Mitch surreptitiously studied Jenny from under lowered lashes. Her face was rosy with excitement, her sapphire eyes sparkling with admiration. She was almost pretty, he decided in surprise. He had not missed the changed appearance, either. Her brown hair was plaited into a French braid and hung midway down her back. A cornflower-blue dress made of gauzy material ended just at her calves, emphasizing her femininity. A concha belt set off her tiny waist to perfection. The sandals she wore were mere scraps of leather made for looks and nothing else.

He experienced an unfamiliar tightening in his chest. His ego would like to think that she had dressed to impress him, but he doubted that, given how she felt about him. The flash of attraction he felt surprised him. At best, she could be called cute, in an odd sort of way. So why should he feel anything at all for her when some of the most attractive women he knew had barely registered with him? The thought was not an appealing one. He didn't want to become entangled with any woman, attractive or not. Past experience had showed him that living the kind of life he led, despite modern conveniences, was too lonely a life for most women.

"Well, have you decided whether you can care for him or not?" His voice came out sounding much gruffer than he had intended.

The smile left Jenny's face. She turned to him, sadness darkening her eyes. "I don't know if we can," she told him softly, continuing to stroke Dynamo's nose. "I have no idea how much it would take to properly care for a horse."

"Aw, Jen!" David pleaded. "Please can't we keep him? I promise I'll take care of him. Renee will help."

"That's enough, David," Mitch told him quietly, watching Jenny's face closely. "It's a big decision and you're not helping matters."

David hung his head and Jenny glared at Mitch. She had opened her mouth to, he felt sure, berate him when David apologized.

"Sorry, Jen," David told her humbly.

"You have nothing to be sorry about," she replied, still glaring at Mitch. "We're a family and we need to make decisions together."

Mitch's lips twitched as he tried to hold back a grin. She seemed to have conveniently forgotten that they were living in Mayer, Arizona, without either her brother's or sister's consent or agreement. As though she could read his thoughts, Jenny's face suffused with color and she quickly looked away.

Dynamo nickered softly, nudging Jenny's shoulder with his nose. As quickly as her anger had surfaced, it disappeared. She stared forlornly into the gelding's dark eyes. Too many thoughts flashed across her face for him to catch, but he didn't miss the longing and it touched him in spite of his intention to remain aloof.

"Look," Mitch told her, "how about I take care of him for you until you can decide for sure whether you want to keep him."

"I can't do that," she told him quietly.

"Why?"

He was annoyed with her inability to make a concrete decision, especially when he felt fairly certain it was because she didn't want to be under obligation to him.

"I can't…well… I just…can't."

"It's no bother to me. I've been caring for him this long, a little longer won't make any difference. If it will make you feel any better, David can earn his board for him by helping me out around here."

He reached out a hand toward the horse, offering a lump of sugar. Dynamo crunched happily, nuzzling Mitch for more. He could see Jenny struggling to make a decision.

She sighed heavily and grudgingly capitulated. "All right."

Mitch released the breath he hadn't even known he was holding.

"If you're sure David won't be a nuisance."

Mitch imperceptibly motioned for David to hold his tongue. "No problem at all."

Chapter 5

Jenny had spent hours preparing the twins for school and working to make their little cabin into a cozy home.

Since jeans seemed to be the one item in their wardrobes they couldn't do without, she'd purchased several pairs for both of them. Pulling out her old sewing machine, she busied herself many hours of the day and night trying to outfit them fashionably but frugally. When she had finished, David was the proud possessor of several Western-style shirts. She had allowed him the coveted pair of cowboy boots, but had drawn the line at the Stetson hat. Nevertheless, David had seemed pleased and excited to be returning to school.

Renee, on the other hand, had become withdrawn and uncommunicative once again. Jenny feared a major setback, but hoped for the best.

Lately she had been spending more time in prayer and often found herself on her knees. Turning things over to the Lord was certainly much easier than trying to cope alone. She found that the more she prayed, the closer she was coming to God again. A new kind of peace had settled into her heart.

Straightening from the sewing machine, she slowly arched her back and stretched her arms above her head. She decided it was time to take a much needed break.

She went into the kitchen and poured herself a glass of iced tea. Surveying the room, she felt a little thrill of pride. New curtains of yellow gingham checks hung from the kitchen windows. Matching place mats graced the table along with cushions for the chairs. A bouquet of desert wildflowers sat perkily in the middle of the table. Sliding a hand to the back of her neck she gently massaged tired muscles. So far it had been hard work, but well worth it.

She glanced at the clock and realized it was almost time to pick David up from Mitch's. Grabbing the car keys, she headed out for the Double A.

When David wasn't occupied with school, he spent most of his free time with Dynamo. Mitch allowed him free rein of the stables as long as he was conscientious enough to leave everything as he found it. Each afternoon he got off the school bus at Mitch's ranch and either Mitch brought him home or Jenny picked him up when he'd finished the chores assigned him as part of his weekly pay. Their agreement seemed to be working out to everyone's advantage.

Jenny pulled into Mitch's driveway and turned off the car. Surprisingly, Renee had assumed her role of student with very little difficulty. She had chosen to remain at the cabin to work on a homework assignment about the Apaches. If David had become enamored of cowboys, Renee was thoroughly fascinated by the Native Americans in the area.

Jenny leaned tiredly against the steering wheel and let the brilliant colors of the sunset soothe her. Normally, David would be waiting for her, but not today. She climbed out of the car and headed for the stables.

Hearing voices at the far end she went in that direction and found Mitch leaning over a newborn foal while David stroked the mother soothingly. Blood covered Mitch's arms to the elbows. Unaware of Jenny's presence, he grinned at David. "Isn't she a beaut?"

David nodded vigorously. "She sure is! Thanks for letting me watch, Mitch. I've never seen a horse born before."

Both man and boy stood silently watching the mother and her foal, a tall cowboy dressed in jeans, T-shirt and boots, and a smaller replica. Jenny couldn't help but smile at the picture they made.

After wiping his hands and arms on a towel, Mitch placed an arm around David's shoulders. David beamed up at him in adoration. The smile left Jenny's face and she had sudden misgivings, wondering just how close David had become to Mitch. This big man had the power to hurt her brother. Still, she didn't want to spoil this moment, so she remained quietly where she stood.

Mitch suddenly looked around and the smile faded from his face. "Looks like we've got company, partner."

Turning, David smiled widely at his sister. He rushed over to her, hair spiked out in all directions. "Guess what, Jen. Mitch and I watched a foal being born. Isn't she pretty?"

She returned his smile, glancing at the foal struggling to rise to its wobbly feet. "She sure is." Addressing herself to Mitch she asked, "What are you going to name her?"

He didn't answer right away. He made sure everything was in order, placing some extra feed in the bin for the mother, then said, "I haven't decided yet." Nodding his head and pointing toward the door, he marshaled them in that direction and flicked off the light behind him.

They walked slowly toward her car. Mitch reached to open the driver's door, waited until Jenny had slid in behind the wheel and then closed it behind her. His eyes traveled slowly over her hair and down around her face. A small smile tugged playfully at the corners of his mouth. "I think I know the perfect name for her," he finally told her. "Maybe I'll call her Jenny Wren."

Jenny wasn't certain he was serious or whether to feel complimented or insulted. Deciding to ignore him, she started the car and put it into gear. When she glanced in her rearview mirror, Mitch was still standing where she had left him.

The merry tones of the *William Tell Overture* warned Jenny of an incoming telephone call. Surprised, she flipped open the phone and clicked the green button.

"Hello?"

"Hi."

She would recognize that lively voice anywhere.

"Hattie! How on earth did you get my number? And how did you know I had a phone, anyway? I just got it this morning."

"I know." She chuckled. "My sister-in-law works for the phone store."

Jenny smiled wryly. "I should have known."

"Anyway, what I'm calling about. I wanted to invite you to have lunch with me. There's someone I want you to meet. Can you meet me at the steak house in about a half hour?"

Since it was Friday and the twins were in school, Jenny readily agreed. She pocketed her phone, picked up her purse and headed out the door, her curiosity aroused.

Jenny walked into the steak house, squinting in the darkness. It took a moment for her eyes to adjust and, by the time they had, Hattie was by her side.

Giving her friend a hug, Hattie towed her along to a table at the back of the restaurant. "I'm so glad you could come."

When they reached the table, Jenny noticed another woman seated there. Her blond hair shimmered in the subdued lighting and her smile was genuine. She wore a pair of faded jeans and a printed T-shirt imprinted with a craft shop logo. She was very attractive and Jenny had to suppress an instant twinge of envy.

She extended her hand toward Jenny, who took it and shook it gently. "Hi. My name's Annie Morrison. Hattie's told me a lot about you."

Jenny quirked an eyebrow at her friend. "Oh? And just what has Hattie been telling you?" Jenny asked, sliding into the vacant seat next to Hattie. She placed her purse next to her chair and leaned her elbows on the table, giving the other woman her attention.

Annie laughed. "Oh, you know Hattie."

"That's what I'm afraid of," Jenny replied, smiling at Hattie.

"You guys! Give me a break. Here I try to do you both a favor and all I get is criticism."

Jenny looked questioningly at both of them. "What kind of favor?"

Before Annie could even open her mouth, Hattie launched into speech. "Well, you see, it's like this. Annie owns a craft shop in Prescott and she's always looking for exciting new crafts."

Looking bemused, Jenny glanced from one to the other. "And? What has this to do with me?"

Annie placed a restraining hand on Hattie's arm. "Please. Allow me." Turning to Jenny, she smiled. "Hattie has been telling me what lovely things you make. She tells me that you're the one who made the beautiful wall hanging in her living room."

Jenny blushed. She had made the hanging for Hattie as a way to say thank you for all that Hattie had done for her and her family. It wasn't much, but it had been made with love.

"She also tells me that you made the beautiful wall hanging that's in the foyer at church."

Throwing Hattie a withering look, Jenny turned back to

Annie. "But what has that to do with a favor? Would you like me to make one for your shop?"

Annie smiled. "I want you to make more than one. I want you to make several."

Jenny's eyes narrowed. "How many rooms are in your shop?"

Hattie burst out laughing. "You don't get it, do you? Annie wants to sell them."

"You would sell them for me?" Jenny asked in surprise.

"I sell lots of crafts for people on consignment."

"Isn't that where you receive some of the money after they sell?"

"Exactly," Annie told her. "You don't pay me anything until they sell, and then I keep a portion of the profits."

"Do you think my wall hangings would sell?"

"I know they would," she said enthusiastically. "Trust me, I know what people like. Your hangings are unusual as well as beautiful."

Jenny's mind began to churn with possibilities. If she could make some money from selling some of her crafts, she could supplement the income she received from the interest on the estate money. That way she might not have to touch as much of the capital. She had no idea how much her crafts would sell for, or for that matter if they would sell at all, but it was worth a try. Up to this point she had tried to be very conservative in her spending. It would be nice to have some fun money.

A waitress approached their table and took their drink order. She returned moments later, placing the drinks on the table.

"Are you ready to order now?" she inquired.

They all three nodded and placed their orders.

"Get what you want, girls," Hattie told them. "I'm buying."

Over lunch Annie told Jenny a little about her shop, the

Lion's Den, and explained how the consignments worked. The asking price for her wall hangings astounded Jenny.

"That much?"

"I assure you, you will get it."

She decided to trust Annie's judgment. After all, the lady evidently knew what she was about. She wouldn't have a successful shop if she didn't.

For the next several days Jenny spent a lot of time visiting department stores in Prescott and searching the internet for supplies she would need to create her wall hangings. Annie had told her that if there were any other crafts she would care to display, she would be more than happy to oblige. As for Jenny, she was thrilled to be able to do the things she loved most. Her hands itched to create beautiful things, but she had not had much time before. Now she could give free rein to her desires and possibly establish an income for herself and the twins.

Jenny decided it was time to return Hattie's car and purchase one of her own. Although she could pay cash if she wanted to, to do so would pretty much deplete her savings account. And since she was unsure what her income would be, she decided it would be best to purchase a good used car and make payments.

Her only problem was that she knew nothing about automobiles and wouldn't know a lemon if it beeped its horn at her. She decided to phone Jacob to see if he would help her find something.

The phone rang several times and she was about to hang up when she heard a deep voice she recognized. "Ameses' residence. May I help you?"

Jenny's fingers curled tightly around the receiver, but surprise rendered her speechless.

"Hello?" he repeated impatiently.

Finding her tongue, Jenny finally managed to squeak out, "I-is Jacob Ames there?"

There followed a slight pause.

"Well, hello, Jenny Wren. If you hang on a minute, I'll get him for you."

Jenny could hear the receiver as it was laid on a table and then voices in the background. Moments later she heard Jacob's hurried voice.

"Jenny? Sorry I couldn't get to the phone quicker, but we were in the pool. What can I do for you?"

"I'm sorry, Jacob. Maybe I should call back later."

"Nonsense. What do you need?"

She explained her dilemma and asked if he would be willing to help her.

"Why don't you just continue to use ours? We're happy to let you," he told her.

"I know, Jacob. But I feel, well… I would just as soon have something I can call my own."

"I understand. Unfortunately, I know little about cars and even less about whether they're mechanically sound. I don't think I'd do you much good." He paused as though thinking. "But I know the perfect person. Mitch knows a lot about mechanical things. He even repairs most of the equipment around his ranch. Let me get him for you."

"Jacob, wait!" Her panicked voice didn't reach him in time. Before she could decide on the best course of action to take, she heard that deep, rumbling voice again.

"So you want to buy a car, huh?" She could hear the laughter in his voice and wondered if he was amused at her or something that Jacob had said to him. "What did you have in mind?"

"I don't know," she told him, peeved at his amusement. "That's why I wanted Jacob's help. I'm not sure what to even look for."

"Well, since it's only about one o'clock, how about I pick you up in an hour and we'll go to Prescott and look. Your best bet would be to try Phoenix, though. We'll see."

"I don't—"

"It's no bother, Jenny Wren," he interrupted.

Why was it that he always made the term Jenny Wren sound almost like an endearment?

"I'll see you soon." He hung up before she could object.

Really! The man was impossible. She still was uncertain about her feelings where he was concerned, but one thing was for certain, whether she would admit it or not, she was excited about seeing him again.

Chapter 6

Jenny watched the approaching blue vehicle somewhat apprehensively. Whatever had she gotten herself into now? And why had Mitch offered to help her select a vehicle, especially when he seemed so ambivalent toward her?

She cringed inwardly, hoping that Mitch didn't think she had requested his help. She felt the hot color warm her cheeks when she thought that he might consider her a gold digger like his former fiancée. She would have to make it clear to him that this hadn't been her idea.

Sliding one hand around the porch upright, she leaned against the pole and took a deep breath. Already the weather had cooled considerably since they had first moved here. Jenny loved it. Warm autumn days, chilly nights. Only the sandy terrain around her remained basically unchanged.

The Jeep came to a halt in front of her. Opening the door, Mitch removed his bulk and strode to the foot of the stairs. He removed his sunglasses and his green eyes narrowed against the sun beneath his perpetual Stetson that, however incongruous it might seem on others, seemed a natural part of him.

At the sight of him, she felt the familiar tightening in her midsection. Ever since that night in her cabin when he had held her in his arms so tenderly, she had had a serious problem erasing him from her mind.

"Hello, Jenny Wren." The softness of his voice sent a thrill charging through her.

"Why do you persist in calling me that? You know that's not my name."

He shrugged his massive shoulders, his eyes raking her up and down. "I don't know. It's what comes to mind whenever I see you. Does it offend you?"

"No…not exactly."

How could she possibly explain to him the conflicting feelings that his use of the term in that throaty voice engendered within her? When she didn't say anything else, he reached for her hand and tugged her down the steps. "Come on. Time's a wastin'."

After stowing her in the passenger seat, he strode to the driver's side, got in and glanced at her briefly before starting the engine. Reaching the end of the driveway, he turned left instead of the more familiar right to Prescott.

"I thought we'd save ourselves some hassle and just go to Phoenix," he told her.

Her eyes widened in surprise and she jerked her head sideways to look at him. "But that's at least an hour's drive one way."

"At least."

"But that will take two hours' driving, not to mention the time it will take to actually look at the cars. You're talking at least four hours!"

"At least," he told her again, and she nearly ground her teeth in irritation.

"I can't be gone that long! The twins will be home in two hours."

He glanced sideways at her. "Don't you think they're old enough to look out for themselves? After all, they'll be thirteen in just a few weeks."

How had he known that? David, probably. "No, I don't think they're old enough to look after themselves and I'd appreciate it if you would just take me back."

"Relax," he said soothingly. "Hattie said she'd watch out for them. She said they could spend the night at her place just in case we got back late."

Why was it that she couldn't be in his company five minutes before she was fighting mad? He absolutely rubbed her the wrong way, especially when he arrogantly took over situations to suit his own needs. It reminded her too much of when Alexander had taken over her life, deciding where they would go, when they would go. The fact that she had willingly allowed it made her cringe when she thought about it now. Never again would she put herself so much under another person's control.

"Who died and left you in charge? I'd like to know." She was struggling to restrain her quick temper, reminding herself that he was merely trying to be helpful. He had no personal interest in her. Surprisingly, that thought didn't cheer her as much as it should have.

"Just because I asked for help doesn't mean I'm helpless," she told him paradoxically. "I don't need anyone to run my life for me."

Mitch's lips twitched with amusement. "Don't you? Do you know what you remind me of? A little, helpless brown mouse, scurrying in every direction just trying to survive. Trying to take care of your family and losing yourself in the process."

She stared at him in utter amazement. Little brown mouse indeed! "How am I risking myself? I'm not in any danger."

"Aren't you, Jenny Wren?"

"Stop calling me that!" she snapped, irritated that he

continually compared her to small, insignificant animals. "If I'm in danger of anything right now, it's blowing my top." She fidgeted nervously with the strap of her seat belt.

Reaching over, Mitch placed a restraining hand over hers.

A constriction formed in her throat and she could hardly breathe. She shook her head in frustration. He had only to touch her and sensible thinking was impossible.

"Calm down," he told her. "I'm merely suggesting that you're losing some of the best years of your life. I'd hate to see your identity swallowed up by worries and responsibilities."

It irked her that he had touched on her one vulnerable point. The one thing she was truly afraid of happening. She wasn't getting any younger. And why did he even care? Pulling her hand from beneath his, she turned to look out the window.

"This area has some very unusual names. Big Bug Creek. Bloody Basin. Do you know how they got them?"

After a moment he placed his hand back on the wheel. Accepting her change of subject, he proceeded to tell her stories of some of the more unusual names. Watching him from under lowered lids, she could see the twitch in his cheek denoting his irritation. Despite the congenial conversation, the atmosphere was decidedly chilly for the rest of the trip.

When they reached Phoenix, he went straight to a popular car dealership. The buzzard symbol they used as their logo was to Jenny inconsistent with their claim of quality merchandise. After all, didn't buzzards eat dead things? Prey on the dying? Somehow this wasn't very reassuring.

Finding nothing there, they went to several more dealerships and all the while Mitch kept up a constant flow of questions and monologue. Jenny felt as though she was very little help. Whenever she would suggest a vehicle she liked, Mitch would invariably have some reason for refusing it. Either it was not built for rough terrain or it was not a good year for that particular model. Some were not heat compatible, some were not mechanically sound. She began to despair that they would ever find something they could agree upon and still fit her budget.

Just when she was about to give up and call it quits, she spotted an older model Toyota Corolla sitting off to the side of the lot. It appealed to her in a curious way. It reminded her of her cabin, sitting there so forlornly just waiting for someone to claim it. She pointed it out to Mitch, not daring to hope he would agree.

He spent some time looking under the hood, checking inside the wheel wells and revving the engine. Lying down, he slid himself underneath the car. After what seemed an inordinate amount of time, he pulled himself out and sat up, shaking his blond hair free of dirt. He tucked his Stetson back on his head and turned to Jenny.

"She looks pretty sound to me. Not too many miles. Hasn't been in an accident."

"How can you tell that?" she asked.

"No marks under the frame." He pulled himself to his feet. "If you like it, it's fine by me. I'd still rather see you in something a little bigger. More solid."

"Bigger and more solid means more gas and more money. This is fine." She turned to the salesman. "What about payments?"

"No problem," he responded. "Why don't you take a test drive and then we'll see what we can work out."

Less than an hour later the salesman handed Jenny the keys to her new car. Well, at least new to her. She patted it lovingly. "You get to come home with me now."

When she looked at Mitch she could see his twitching lips. She flushed all the way to the roots of her hair. He must think her an absolute nutcase, but what did it matter? She swelled with pride. She owned her very first car for the very first time in her life. It gave her a feeling of independence, as if she were more the master of her own destiny.

It suddenly occurred to her that instead of driving back with Mitch, she would be driving back on her own. Despite her avowal of independence, she felt somewhat shaken at the thought.

"Is it all right if I follow you home? I don't think I can remember how to get there on my own."

"Well, of course you'll follow me home," Mitch told her impatiently. He glared at her. "Did you really think I'd leave you on your own?"

How was she supposed to know any different? She barely knew the man! She pressed her lips tightly together to keep venomous words from spilling forth. Really, he could be so aggravating.

Mitch turned to the salesman. "Is it all right if we leave the car here for a while?"

"Sure. As long as you want, only we close at nine."

"We should be back by then," Mitch told him. "If not, it should be safe here in the parking lot."

"Where are we going?" Jenny asked.

"I thought I'd take you to supper. There's a restaurant close by I think you might enjoy. If that's okay with you?"

She supposed she should get home. After all, it would still take them an hour to get there. He had said that Hattie would look after the twins, but did she really want to go to dinner with Mitch? Somehow she didn't think it would be a good idea to spend too much time in the man's company, but he was looking at her in a way that made it seem as though he really did want to spend time with her. Her mind told her one thing, but her heart was behaving in a much sillier way.

"I'd like that," she agreed.

Her heart reacted even sillier as a slow smile spread across his features. Placing a hand behind her back, he guided her to the Jeep and helped her inside.

He took her to an expensive restaurant at the top of the Hyatt Regency Hotel, where they rapidly ascended the twenty-six floors in a glass-enclosed express elevator. Her stomach was still trying to catch up when the door slid open. She and Mitch stepped off with several other people and Jenny took time to look around.

"Table for Anderson," she heard Mitch tell the maître d'.

He glanced quickly down his list before leading them to their seat. Jenny was impressed with the elegance of the atmosphere, although it seemed tables had been crowded into every available space. The restaurant was round and it was some time before she realized that it was revolving.

They were seated next to a window and Jenny marveled at the view. Buildings spread out in all directions as far as the eye could see. The only thing that seemed to stop their sprawling expansion was the surrounding mountains visible in the distance.

The waiter brought their menus and crystal glasses of water with lemon slices floating in their depths.

"Can I get you something to drink?" he inquired.

Mitch raised an eyebrow, querying her decision.

"I'll have a cola, please," she answered, smiling at the waiter.

"And for you, sir?"

"The same."

"Very good. I'll return in a moment with your drinks and take your order."

Jenny watched him walk away, a sudden feeling of shyness overcoming her. She glanced uncomfortably at Mitch only to find him watching her, his expression thoughtful.

"I want to thank you for helping me," she told him, trying to relieve some of the awkwardness she was experiencing. "I wouldn't have known anything about finding a car."

He inclined his head slightly, a sudden grin slicing across his face. "Maybe you could have just talked to the cars. Surely one of them would have helped you."

It reminded her that he had heard her talking to her little car. The red of her silky blouse couldn't compete with her face. Instead of being offended, she chose to answer him lightly.

"I know it's crazy, but growing up with Disney has a tendency to warp your vision of reality. I've always felt guilty whenever I thought I might be neglecting an object or an animal's feelings." She smiled. "I know it's crazy, but…what can I say?"

The waiter arrived to take their orders. He set their drinks in front of them and smilingly turned to Jenny.

"Have you had time to decide?"

The menu contained a very limited selection and the prices were somewhat expensive. Knowing that Mitch could easily afford it and wouldn't have brought her here unless he'd wanted to, she still had trouble choosing from such a costly selection. Her frugal nature rebelled at such extravagance. Knowing that this was likely to be the only time she would dine here, she decided to splurge.

"I'll have the prime rib," she answered, handing him back the menu. Mitch chose the same. After the waiter had left, Mitch turned back to her.

"See those mountains over there?" He pointed out the clear glass window to some peaks in the distance. "They're called the Superstitions. And believe me there are enough superstitions about those mountains that they deserve the name. Supposedly, they contain the Lost Dutchman's Mine."

The deep rumble of his voice calmed her earlier apprehension. For the time being, they seemed to have put their animosity toward each other aside.

"What is the Lost Dutchman's Mine? Was it a gold mine?"

"Exactly. Supposedly in the 1800s a Dutchman named Jacob Waltz found a gold mine in those mountains. He was murdered and no one has ever been able to find the location."

"Do people still try? I mean, do people still pan for gold today?"

"Sure thing. Mining is one of Arizona's largest industries, in one form or another. Although copper is by far the largest product extracted."

When their meal arrived Jenny thoroughly enjoyed it. Mitch kept up a continuous flow of conversation, drifting from one subject to another. Jenny relaxed, her pleasure making her eyes sparkle. Mitch was an amusing companion when he chose to be. In fact, he was quite charming.

By the time they left the restaurant, it was well past nine o'clock. Jenny was concerned about her new car, though Mitch assured her there would be no problem. Driving back to the dealership, Mitch was unusually quiet. She was beginning to get edgy, racking her brains for a suitable topic of conversation. Everything that occurred to her seemed rather inane.

Finally, taking his eyes off the road, he glanced briefly at her before concentrating once again on the traffic.

"You really like living here, don't you? I mean, it doesn't bother you to live in the desert relatively isolated from most conveniences."

Jenny was surprised. She looked over at him, a slight frown puckering her brow. This was not just some rhetorical question thrown out for conversation's sake. Her intuition told her that for some reason her answer was important to him.

"I love it," she told him simply. "I wouldn't want to live anywhere else."

His look was doubtful. "You don't hanker after the bright lights? The excitement of a big city such as Phoenix maybe?"

Watching the traffic through the windshield even at this late hour, she wondered how he could even ask such a question. Visiting Phoenix might be fun once in a while, but she could never live there. Shaking her head she told him, "I have everything I want where I'm at. What more could I ask for?"

"A job, perhaps?" he queried mildly. "Surely the money from the estate can't last forever."

Was he hinting at buying her property again?

For some reason she was reluctant to apprise him of her changed circumstances. As of yet she had received no money from the sale of her crafts, although Annie had informed her that everything was going well. She would receive a check once a month from the Lion's Den for her part of the sales, but she had a couple of weeks to wait yet. It was hard for her to believe that what she sold would bring in very much money.

"Things will work out," she told him.

Arriving at the dealership parking lot, they found the place closed. Her car, however, was sitting toward the back of the lot under a brightly shining light. Jenny got out her keys and climbed inside.

"Do you have your papers?" Mitch asked her.

Reaching into her purse, she pulled out the papers and handed them to him.

"I'll just let the security guard know so he doesn't think we're stealing the car."

When Mitch returned, he leaned down and she rolled down her window.

"Be sure you stay close behind me. If for some reason we get separated, I'll pull off the road and wait for you. Okay?"

She nodded, clutching the wheel nervously. For her part, she determined that there would be no chance of that happening. She was going to stick to him like proverbial glue.

"Stay close."

She watched him slide into his Jeep before starting her car. Her hands were shaking slightly and she threw a fleeting prayer upward for their safety. Although she trusted

Mitch completely, her driving left a lot to be desired. In fact, she had only had her driver's license a few years. There had been no necessity living on a farm and later, living in a college dorm made it unnecessary to have transportation since everything had been within walking distance.

Despite the lateness of the hour, the freeway between Phoenix and Mayer was heavy with traffic. It was almost ten-thirty when Jenny parked her car in her yard beside Mitch's Jeep. He pulled her door open before she had the chance and helped her out. He held her hand for a long time, finally releasing it when she gave a slight tug.

"I enjoyed myself tonight," he told her, his throaty voice causing those cartwheels in her stomach again.

"I did, too. Thank you for taking me."

"My pleasure." He was looking at her in a way no man ever had before and it made warmth ripple across her in waves.

"I'm having a barbecue next Saturday," he told her. "I'd like you to come. David and Renee, also."

Jenny hesitated. His earlier animosity toward her seemed to have dissipated, but was he only being polite? Tonight, for the first time since she had met him, she felt as though they might just be able to put the past behind them and be friends.

"I'll have to ask David and Renee."

"By all means," he agreed. "Just don't use them as an excuse not to come."

Really? Did he have to go there? Jenny's temper flared instantly. "I'll have you know, I don't hide behind my brother and sister. I don't have to. If I want to come, I'll come. And if I don't want to, I won't."

She knew she sounded childish. He must have thought so, as well, because instead of getting angry, his lips twitched and, reaching out a hand, he stroked a gentle finger down her cheek. Her mind told her to go inside before the feelings he engendered in her could become something more complicated, but her feet were rooted to the spot.

His hand curled around the back of her neck and he tugged her forward until their lips were mere inches apart. He was obviously giving her the chance to object but although one part of her mind cried out for her to do so, the other part knew that it was too late.

His kiss began as a gentle exploration, deepening when she responded. When he finally released her, she could hardly breathe and her legs felt like jelly.

"Will you come to the barbecue?" he asked huskily.

Her mind was too numb to deny him.

"We'll come," she answered just as huskily.

He had to lean forward to catch the words and his eyes gleamed. Releasing her, he retreated to his Jeep, pausing before sliding inside.

"Go inside and turn on the light. I want to make sure you're okay."

Unlocking the door, Jenny quickly disappeared inside.

Driving home Mitch continually chastised himself. What on earth had prompted him to kiss her, for crying out loud? He could still feel the warmth of her in his arms, making his heart pound furiously. He had never intended to go that far, but staring into those enticing eyes had sent his common sense somewhere beyond retrieval.

Her kiss had convinced him that she was attracted to him, as well. She had been tentative at first, but then she had given herself up to the same feelings that had been coursing through him. It had taken a great effort to put a brake on that scene, or he might have said or done something he would have later regretted.

What surprised him was how right it had felt. He couldn't ever remember anything having felt so right before. Even with Amanda. With her, he had been attracted to her physical beauty; the same couldn't be said of Jenny. With Jenny, it was something more elemental.

Amanda's beauty had incited physical desire, whereas holding Jenny in his arms had made him feel protective. Strong. As though he could slay any number of dragons.

Sighing, he leaned his head back against the seat. This feeling was nothing close to what he had experienced with Amanda. She had been so beautiful and he had been so young. He had wanted her more than anything in the world, until he'd realized how shallow she was. Physical desire had quickly diminished in the face of her selfishness.

He had been struggling against these encroaching feelings for Jenny since the first moment he had laid eyes on her, which had caused him to, at times, be harsher than he should have been.

First his mother, then Amanda. He never wanted to trust another woman again. He had believed himself to be immune from such attraction. Vaccinated by pain.

But Jenny. So sweet. So trusting. Giving of herself so unselfishly. Or was she as innocent as she seemed? She needed money and he had that in abundance. He had been fooled before. Was he following down that same path again?

Somehow, he had to put a brake on his thoughts and feelings before things got out of hand. Pulling into his driveway, he snorted softly. That was going to be easier said than done.

Chapter 7

Jenny was calling herself all kinds of a fool as she headed down the dirt road toward Mitch's ranch. The cool breeze lifted the curls away from her forehead, where an unattractive frown resided. Every time she thought about the night Mitch had brought her home from Phoenix, she squirmed a little in the seat.

Why had he kissed her? Was it even remotely possible that he could be developing feelings for her, or was it some kind of ruse to get her to sell her ranch to him? Or was it something even more basic than that? She *was* the only single woman around for miles. Was she, as she had been with Alexander, something to play with until something better came along? That kiss had left her more shaken than she cared to admit, and she didn't like feeling so vulnerable again.

Dreams aside, the cold light of day had restored her normally levelheaded disposition. If she allowed herself to become emotionally involved, she was just asking for trouble. She had learned about Mitch's past from Hattie and, although he was certainly no misogynist, he would protect his own heart at all costs. The only one who would be hurt by such a one-sided relationship would be her.

And now here she was about to beard the lion in his den. Surely she must be a masochist or something. She had decided to treat him coolly at church, which had turned out to be a waste of effort since his coolness had far exceeded hers, showing her that he regretted his action, as well.

If it hadn't been for David and Renee she would have found an excuse not to attend the barbecue. But David had disappeared early this morning when Mitch had stopped by to pick him up, making it necessary for her to retrieve him from Mitch's ranch.

Her mind was jerked back to the present when Renee screamed.

"Stop! Jen, stop!"

Slamming on the brakes, the car skidded sideways toward the shoulder of the road. Renee already had her hand on the handle and was jerking open the door. Heart pounding, Jenny watched in the rearview mirror as Renee ran back along the road, her movements urgent.

Climbing from the vehicle, she followed on unsteady legs. "Don't ever do that again!" she remonstrated harshly. "What do you see?"

It was several seconds before Jenny could see past Renee's bent form and noticed some sort of animal lying on the side of the road. When Renee would have reached out to touch it, Jenny quickly pulled her back.

"Don't touch it!"

"But it's just a puppy, Jen. It's hurt. It needs help."

From the look of it, the puppy needed more than she was equipped to offer. Ratty brown fur was mingled with blood across its backside. Its little pink tongue hung forlornly from the side of its mouth. A soft whine escaped its throat and Renee pulled away from Jenny's restraining hand, kneeling beside it.

"We have to do something!" she protested. "We can't just leave it here."

If they left it here there was no telling what might happen to it. It was possible they wouldn't even be able to find the same spot on this stretch of road. Worse yet, either the coyotes or buzzards might take it away. It was amazing that they hadn't found the poor thing already.

Squinting her eyes against the sun, Jenny thought she could detect black shapes circling above their heads even now. Shivering, she turned back to the puppy.

"We'll just have to take him to Mitch's with us. He might be able to do something."

She could remember the night he had helped to deliver the colt. Mitch seemed to know a lot about caring for animals, and he seemed to genuinely care about their welfare.

"Go get the blanket from the trunk of the car," she directed Renee as she knelt beside the trembling ball of brown fur.

Seconds later the blanket was thrust into her hand. Turning to Renee she enjoined her to get in the car while she carefully lifted the puppy. "I'll put him in your lap."

A sudden yelp made her hesitate. It was possible that she would injure the puppy even more than he already was if she moved him, but she sure couldn't leave it here. She would just have to hope for the best.

Constant little whimpers came from the blanketed bundle as she hurried toward the car. Laying the puppy gently on Renee's lap, she told her, "Hang on tight, but try not to hurt him."

Jenny drove down the dirt road like a maniac, dust scattering along behind her. The puppy seemed unusually quiet now. Worried that it might have already died, Jenny glanced at the white, set face of her sister and prayed not. Renee's gentle heart would be broken. As though she read Jenny's mind, Renee offered up a strained little prayer.

"Please, Lord. Don't let him die."

Skidding to a halt in Mitch's driveway, Jenny threw open the door and slammed it behind her. "Stay put. I'll see if I can find Mitch."

It didn't take Jenny long to spot Mitch. He stood head and shoulders above nearly everyone in the crowd, although Stetsons abounded throughout the grassy area. Barely pausing, Jenny pushed her way forward, ignoring Hattie's rapidly waving arms.

Reaching his side, she placed an urgent hand on his arm. He glanced down, his face at once becoming a hard mask. "So, you're speaking to me today, are you?"

At his icy tone, she jerked her hand away. Everything considered, she supposed she deserved the rebuke, although she considered it was a little more the pot calling the kettle black.

Jenny sighed impatiently. She had neither the time nor the inclination to go into this with him now. "I need your help."

His face was instant attention. "It must be something important if you're asking for *my* help." He glanced behind her. "Where's Renee? Did something happen to Renee?" he asked anxiously.

"She's in the car..."

Grabbing her arm, Mitch strode toward the front of the house. Since he was in a hurry she had to run to keep up with him, too breathless to protest. Rounding the corner, he spotted Renee sitting in the car. Even from that distance it was obvious she was in distress. Her cheeks were wet with tears.

Letting go of Jenny, Mitch rapidly covered the rest of the distance without her. Jenny could hear his gentle voice as she approached, but she couldn't make out the words. Renee started babbling and pointing to her lap. By the time

Jenny arrived, Mitch had taken control. He was kneeling beside the open door and was studying the pup, going over it with gentle hands.

"I don't think anything's broken. Looks like he might have been hit by a car." When he touched the pup's hindquarters it let out a meager yelp. "Muscles are probably bruised. The tendons may be strained. I need to clean him up a bit before I can tell for sure."

Reaching down, he gently lifted the puppy from Renee's lap, blanket and all. He barely glanced at Jenny before he strode away. Renee got out of the car and ran to catch up with him. Jenny watched them walk away, a sinking feeling in the pit of her stomach. Well, what had she expected? The way she had treated Mitch the past week, it was a wonder he was speaking to her at all.

Jenny chose to join the party by the pool rather than follow Mitch and Renee. It was obvious she wasn't needed. Feeling more than a little sorry for herself, she wound her way through the guests, greeting people she knew as she went along. When she reached Hattie's side, Hattie placed a cool drink in her hand.

"I saw you arrive," she told her. "What's happened? I watched you and Mitch disappear and now you return alone looking like you lost your last friend."

Jenny took a sip of the lemonade, hoping that it would help remove the knot that seemed to have formed in her throat.

"On the way here, Renee spotted an injured puppy alongside the road. We brought it here. Renee is with Mitch now. I think they went to the stables."

"Probably." Hattie nodded. "Mitch has a dispensary of sorts there."

Hattie pulled Jenny along as she mingled with the other guests. Most of the people Jenny recognized from church. A few she had never seen before.

Jenny noticed a woman standing off to the side. Artificially colored platinum-blond hair was coiled into a French twist. Her makeup was applied skillfully so as to give the allusion of being natural. Her clinging blue silk dress hugged her body, showing off her excellent figure to its best advantage. For some reason Jenny felt instant antipathy toward the stunning creature. Surely she wasn't envious. She had met enough ravishing beauties in her time who hadn't caused the least little twinge. But something about this woman stirred a mixture of feelings inside, and none of them were very Christian.

"Who's that?"

Hattie followed her look, the smile on her face freezing into place. "What's *she* doing here?"

The other woman noticed Hattie and made her way to their side.

"Hello, Hattie."

"Amanda. What brings you to the back of beyond? Does Mitch know you're here?"

"Heavens, yes. He invited me."

The tension between the two women was so thick it could have been cut with the proverbial knife. Reluctantly, Hattie introduced Jenny.

So this was the infamous Amanda, the foolish woman who gave up a life with Mitch here on this beautiful ranch to be near the bright lights of the city. Before she could comment, Mitch joined the group. He nodded to each woman before turning to Jenny.

"We cleaned the pup up as best we could under the circumstances." His voice was clipped. Cool. "He should survive, but I wouldn't advise moving him right now. Renee, however, seems to disagree with me. She wants to take him home tonight. Perhaps you can talk some sense into her." Taking Jenny by the arm, he walked her away from the group. "Excuse us, ladies."

That he seemed to be only mildly polite to the blonde

beauty seemed to cause Hattie some sense of satisfaction. She called after Jenny, "I'll talk to you later."

Jenny tried to pry Mitch's fingers from her arm, but he only tightened his grip. "You're hurting me."

The pressure was instantly loosened although his fingers remained firmly around her arm. "That's nothing compared with what I'd like to do to you," he growled.

She glanced up at him in surprise but wisely refrained from comment. Anger simmered just beneath his civilized exterior and she had no desire to be the one who brought it to a boil.

When they reached the stables he turned right, entering a small office to the side. Everything was in pristine condition, the chrome gleaming brightly on utensils placed strategically throughout the room. Renee sat next to the examining table, gently stroking the puppy, though it was hardly recognizable. It had been cleaned fairly well, and was trying to sit up. Renee laughed as it reached up and, taking her by surprise, licked her chin. Jenny noticed a reluctant smile tug at Mitch's lips. The hardness left his eyes and, walking across the room, he placed an arm around Renee's shoulders.

"See, Mitch," she told him. "He's better already. Can't I please take him home?" Spotting Jenny, she turned her arguments to the one she considered carried more weight in the decision. "Please, Jen. I'll be very careful and I'll take really good care of him."

Jenny refused to look at Mitch. "What did Mitch say?"

Renee's shoulders drooped. "He says that the pup should stay here in case he develops an infection." Her eyes were pleading. "But I don't think that will happen. Not if I take very good care of him."

Walking over to the table, Jenny reached a gentle finger down to stroke the pup's head. He playfully nipped her. She could almost swear that it was smiling. The haggard-looking lump of fur they had brought here had changed dramatically. It was still far too thin, but good, nourishing food would soon cure that. She smiled at Renee before looking up at Mitch.

"Did I hear you say *he?*" He was watching her with interest, though his eyes remained fathomless pools of green. He nodded his head slightly, still saying nothing.

"Is there really a chance that he'll develop an infection?"

"There's always the chance that an infection will result from as severe an injury as this, but I gave him an antibiotic."

She sighed as Renee continued to watch her with those pleading blue eyes. "I suppose if something happened we could give you a call?" It was more a question than a statement.

Blowing out an aggravated breath, Mitch stared at her a long time before he answered, "I can see that neither one of you is going to be sensible about this." He raked his hand through his hair, skewing it to the side. "Yes, you can call me anytime." The look he gave Renee was much more tolerant than any he had given Jenny heretofore.

"Now, why don't you go see if you can find David and tell him all about it?" he told Renee. "He's around here somewhere."

As Renee got up to leave, she lovingly stroked the puppy. "I'll be right back," she told him.

Jenny watched her leave with something akin to panic. The last thing she wanted was to be alone with Mitch. She hastily made to follow when Mitch reached out and pushed the door closed, effectively blocking her only escape route.

"Oh, no, you don't," he told her. "You and I have some talking to do. I've been trying to talk to you all week, but you keep avoiding me. Not anymore."

The puppy yipped and Jenny was relieved to have somewhere to turn her attention. Seeing Mitch's set expression was unnerving, to say the least.

"I'm sorry. What did you want to say?"

Heaving a sigh, he closed the distance between them. When he reached out to her, she flinched away, and the anger that had been simmering beneath the surface exploded like a volcano.

"What's wrong with you? The other night—"

"The other night was the other night," she interrupted. "It was a mistake. What more is there to say?"

"There's a whole lot more to say!" he snapped.

"I'd rather forget it, if you don't mind." As if that was going to happen. It was a beautiful moment forever imbedded in her memory. She just couldn't bear it if he apologized.

He went absolutely still, his eyes narrowing with his thoughts. "If that's the way you want it."

She dug her fingers softly into the puppy's fur. A slight wag of his scruffy tail acknowledged the caress.

"I do," she told him softly.

"Jenny—" A banging on the door interrupted him. She could hear him grind his teeth in frustration.

"Those twins have the worst timing," he practically growled. He reached behind him, jerking open the door.

Only it wasn't the twins. Amanda stood at the door, her red lips curling up into a smile. "What's keeping you, darling? I need to get home."

Mitch froze, his face creasing in irritation. He glanced in frustration from Jenny to Amanda and back again. "I'm sorry, Amanda. I was trying to clear up some business with Jenny."

She gave Jenny a curious look. "About selling her ranch?"

Before Mitch could answer, Jenny had picked up the puppy, despite his yelping protest, and fled past them out the door.

"Thanks for the help," she told him without looking at him. "You can send me a bill."

"Jenny, wait!"

He made a move to follow her but Amanda was blocking the doorway. Jenny could hear her voice as she rounded the corner.

"I'm sorry, Mitch. Did I say something wrong?"

Fortunately, Jenny didn't have to go far to look for David and Renee. They almost collided with her as she turned the corner.

"Come on," she told them, not waiting to see if they obeyed. When she reached the car they were right behind her.

"Are you all right, Jen?" David asked her. "Your face is awfully white."

"I'm fine, David. Just get in the car."

Both hurried to comply. When Jenny used that particular tone of voice, they knew she meant business.

Braking with a flourish in front of their cabin, Jenny turned to Renee. No one had uttered a single word for the entire twenty-minute journey. Jenny was aware of the curious looks her siblings were giving her, but she wasn't about to hurt their opinion of a man who had been nothing but kind to them.

"Take the puppy inside, Renee. I'll see if I can find a box or something to put it in to make it comfortable. David, warm a little milk and we'll see if we can get him to eat something."

The twins did as commanded, carefully carrying the blanket between them like a stretcher, but Jenny's mind was only half on the job at hand. Was it possible that Mitch had thought to seduce her to get her to sell the ranch to him? That thought made more sense to her than believing he could be attracted to her, especially if he had taken up with Amanda again. The woman had been foolish to leave such a man for imagined pleasures elsewhere.

Mitch's mother had left his father for the same reason. Was that why he had questioned her so intently about wanting to live in the city? Frankly, Jenny considered both women fools. But had Mitch been trying to see if she would succumb to the delights of big-city living? Was that why he had taken her to the Compass Room, where she could see the brilliant lights of the great metropolitan area?

And what did all of this have to do with her ranch? Had he hoped to elicit a desire in her to leave and sell him the ranch, and then, when that hadn't worked, thought that he could make her fall in love with him? Perhaps he had thought the plain little farm girl would be thrilled by the attention. As Alexander had.

That thought stiffened her backbone. She had a family to think of. She needed to cast off any thoughts of a romantic nature and focus on the job at hand. She was no longer a young, foolish schoolgirl looking for acceptance. She was a woman with responsibilities.

If only it were that easy to convince her heart.

Mitch slammed his palm against the porch rail, oblivious to the pain that winged its way up his arm. How could he have been so stupid? Jenny was avoiding him big-time. The hurt look on her face yesterday would stay with him forever. Why had he invited Amanda, anyway? Because he'd wanted to prove something to himself, that's why. He was trying to fathom the depth of his feelings for one little Jenny Wren.

Ever since he had met Jenny, he had been fighting a battle within himself. Feelings he hadn't known he possessed were surfacing and he was unsure just what to do with them. One moment he believed himself involved, the next he decided he was imagining things. One minute Jenny was sweet and warm, the next she was as cold as a glacier.

What a mistake it had been to invite Amanda to the barbecue. When her brother had informed him that she was going to be in town for the barbecue, Mitch had decided that perhaps he should invite her. Just to see if there were any feelings left.

It hadn't taken him five minutes in her company to know that any feelings he might have had were long dead. Ashes in the wind.

Mitch realized that what he had once thought was love had merely been physical attraction. Amanda was still as beautiful as ever, but that beauty no longer appealed to him. He wanted something much more now. He wanted someone who could share his spiritual life as well as his physical one.

From the first moment he had met Jenny, he had been unwillingly attracted to her. Although he had at first thought that she was a rather plain little thing, he had since revised his opinion. Clear, honest, bright blue eyes had stared out at him from a creamy complexion with the barest hint of makeup. Soft brown hair curled becomingly around her shoulders. Her grace and poise were obvious in her every movement. The difference between Amanda and Jenny in looks was more than made up for in personality. The saying about beauty being in the eye of the beholder was one he could definitely relate to now. Jenny might not be a great beauty, but she had grown on him until he felt compelled to find out just how deep those feelings ran.

One kiss from Jenny had shaken him to his core and left him with little doubt. His determination to remain uncommitted had been scattered to the four winds.

Mitch smiled wryly. He had it bad. If he'd had any doubts before, they had vanished completely now. But now, how could he undo the damage wrought by Amanda's sudden appearance. Amanda's untimely entrance at the barn had spoiled his chance to explain things to Jenny and to try to find out if her feelings were anywhere near as complicated as his. By the time he had managed to get away from Amanda and out to the driveway, Jenny's little car was fast disappearing down the drive.

Since then, she had avoided him at every opportunity. He felt irritated all over again when he thought about it. The only thing he knew to do was to give her some time.

Sighing, he turned and went inside.

Chapter 8

"Are you sure you wouldn't want to sell that one?" Annie Morrison asked as she stared up at the wall hanging in Jenny's living room. "The earth tones are wonderful and blend so well with your rustic decor."

Jenny smiled. "That's exactly why I don't wish to part with it. I made it especially for this room, to help make it homier. Know what I mean?"

"I suppose," Annie's voice seemed slightly deflated.

"I could make another one that's similar, but I prefer not to make two alike."

"I understand. That's the artist in you."

"Well, I don't know about that."

Annie returned to her seat across from Jenny. "You're too modest, you know. I don't think you are really aware of your own potential."

"You're serious. You really think I have that much talent?"

"Trust me. You have remarkable talent, and it's only beginning to surface."

Jenny stared across at her friend. Since Annie had begun to sell Jenny's crafts they had seen a lot of each other. Annie and Hattie were best of friends, but no two people could be more different. Where Hattie was quick and impulsive, Annie's impulses were more inclined to be temperate. Annie gave things a lot of thought.

The more Jenny spent time with Annie, the more she grew to love her. Having met Annie's fiancé, Jenny was prepared to believe the saying that opposites attract. Jeremy was as different from Annie as night was from day.

"I can't believe you never did much artwork before," Annie repeated for the hundredth time.

Jenny shrugged. "I never really had the time. Oh, I made things for my family and friends, but most of my time was spent caring for farm animals and then trying to excel in college. And then working and taking care of the twins. I must admit, I'm thrilled to be able to satisfy my creative urges."

"You've certainly brought my shop a lot of business since I started selling your work."

Jenny glanced at the check she held in her hand. "I can't believe how much this is. Are you sure you took out your commission?"

"Honey, I'm generous, but not that generous. If I didn't take my part to pay the bills, there wouldn't be a shop left to sell other people's creations. I assure you, you earned it."

Jenny laid the check on the coffee table, shaking her head.

"I still can't believe it."

"Well, believe it."

"Can I get you something to drink? Coffee? Tea? A cola?" asked Jenny as she rose to her feet.

"Please. A cola would be great. Then there are some things I'd like to discuss with you."

Jenny raised an eyebrow inquiringly.

"Business things," Annie told her. "So we'll make ourselves comfortable first."

Jenny grinned to herself. Right to the point. In that way, Hattie and Annie were a lot alike. Pouring them each a drink, Jenny returned to the living room. She placed Annie's drink on a coaster and laid a paper napkin beside it. Seating herself, she looked at Annie expectantly.

"Well, go ahead. I'm all ears."

"Well, for starters I didn't come all this way just to bring your check, although I was glad to do it. I wanted to know if you have any more crafts ready to be sold."

"As a matter of fact, I do." Jenny was a little surprised. "Do you mean to say that you've sold all the others?"

"Most of them. I was hoping we could work out an arrangement where you could get your crafts to me a little more quickly. I know it's a long way from here to Prescott, but I thought we should decide how often and when."

"How often would you suggest?"

"That depends on you," Annie told her. "How much can you do, and how often?"

Jenny thought hard before answering. "Well, the cabin's in good shape now, and since the twins are in school I'm not as busy as I was before. I like to be available in the evenings to help them with their homework and fix supper."

Annie smiled. "You'd make a wonderful wife. I have a feeling Jeremy will be eating lots of TV dinners after we're married."

"Pshaw!" Jenny scoffed. "I don't believe that for a moment. You're much too organized."

Placing her glass on the coaster, Annie leaned forward. "There's something else you might like to consider. It might be best for you if you considered selling this place and buying a place in Prescott."

Jenny stared at her in horror. "Leave here?" She shook her head slowly from side to side. "I couldn't. You have no idea what this place means to me."

"I think I do, but consider all the benefits of living closer to a larger town. Not that Prescott is so large, but it's getting there."

Jenny said nothing. There was no way she could explain just what this place really meant to her. She didn't understand it herself. She only knew that she felt more at home here than anyplace she had ever lived, including the farm in North Dakota.

"We love it here," she told Annie simply. "I don't think I could ever get the twins to agree to leave."

"Well, give it some thought, anyway."

Over the next several days Jenny did give it some thought. She wavered back and forth between feeling selfish at not wanting to leave and being sure she was right in *not* moving. Was she being fair to the twins? She had avoided talking about it with them, but sometime soon she knew she would have to. She wanted to be fair. It took time and money to go to Prescott every time she needed craft supplies, but she used the opportunity to take finished products to Annie.

Jenny placed David's birthday present in a box and carefully wrapped it in cowboy-print wrapping paper. David's was easy. It was Renee she was having a problem buying for. David was open with his wants and desires, but Renee was still reluctant about opening herself up.

She had finally decided to make Renee several outfits. Her taste in clothes had changed considerably since they'd moved here. For all of her teasing David about wanting to dress Western, it seemed Renee's tastes were leaning in that direction a lot lately, also. She wondered if it had something to do with Mark Ames.

The phone interrupted her thoughts and she was still smiling as she flipped it open.

"Hello? Jenny Gordon here."

"Hi, Jenny. Hattie here." A giggle from the other end of the line caused Jenny's smile to widen into a grin.

"I like your new way of answering the phone," Hattie told her. "Much more dignified."

"I'm glad you approve."

"Anyway, I have something I want to discuss with you. It's about David and Renee."

The smile left Jenny's face. "What about David and Renee?"

"Oh it's nothing bad," Hattie hastened to assure her. "I just wanted to find out what you're going to do for their birthday?"

"I…I was just going to have cake and give them their presents." Jenny was mystified. It hadn't occurred to her to invite anyone else since their ranch was so far from their friends.

"I have a better idea," Hattie said excitedly. "How about having a birthday picnic in Dewey?"

"In Dewey?" Jenny was becoming more mystified by the minute.

"Let me explain. Every year Young's Farm has a pumpkin festival. Everyone from around here goes. So I thought if we could call some of David's and Renee's friends, we could all meet there at a particular time and have a picnic somewhere in the vicinity. Then we could all go over to Young's Farm and spend some time looking around."

"That sounds like fun!"

"I think so. All we need is someone to bring the birthday cake and we'll have everyone bring something for the picnic lunch."

"I'll do the cake," Jenny told her, getting excited.

"I was hoping you'd say that. How about I make all the arrangements with everyone and that way you don't have to worry about David and Renee getting wind of it."

"That's an awful lot of work."

"No problem. Haven't you figured out by now that I'm a workaholic?"

"I sometimes get that impression," Jenny told her, smiling.

"Anyway, I'll get back to you with all the details. Right now I have some lists to make, some people to call, some shopping to do…"

"Okay! Okay, I get the picture. I'll talk to you later. And…Hattie?"

"Yes?"

"Thanks."

Hattie laughed. "Anytime. Besides, I love parties."

Jenny was chuckling as she hung up the phone. Hattie was a wonderful friend and a wonderful Christian. She didn't just speak Christianity, she actually lived it. The only time Jenny could ever remember seeing Hattie less than charitable was when she'd been around Amanda. The fact that Amanda had hurt one of Hattie's best friends had made her less than congenial toward the woman. Not that she could blame Hattie.

For the next several days Hattie and Jenny spent a lot of time on the phone, plotting. They agreed on an area to have the picnic and decided on a time. Everything seemed to be going smoothly. David and Renee didn't suspect anything, and Jenny was sure it was because they realized how hard it would be for their friends to come to the ranch. Jenny smiled secretly to herself. This was fun. She was glad Hattie had thought of it.

Their birthday arrived and to keep them from being disappointed or maybe conjecturing about birthday plans, Jenny decided to have a small party at the ranch. Just the three of them.

She pulled their favorite chocolate cake from the oven and set it on the counter to cool. The larger cake she had made yesterday was safely tucked away at Hattie's. She glanced out the kitchen window. The days were much cooler now in October. A stillness seemed to have settled over the land, the precursor of winter dormancy.

The sky was a heavenly blue, with white billowy clouds floating lazily across it. She had been told that sometimes in the winter, Mayer would receive snow. She shook her head in disbelief. It was hard to imagine, remembering the hundred-degree temperatures of summer.

It worried her a little. Already it was cold when they woke up in the mornings. What would it be like when winter really set in? Cousin Tito hadn't had air-conditioning installed, nor had he had heat. The fireplace was the only source of heat in the cabin.

If that was their only way to have heat, then somehow she would have to manage to get some firewood. But where did one get firewood in the middle of the desert? Shrugging these thoughts away, she pulled out the cocoa to make the frosting. She would worry about that later. Right now she had two siblings to please.

The cake was no surprise to either of the twins since it was Saturday and they had wandered in and out of the kitchen all day.

"I'm bored," David told her. "Why can't I go to Mitch's?"

"I told you. I thought we'd have a birthday party. Just the three of us."

Renee gave her brother a withering glare. "Don't be a dink," she told him. "Jenny's worked hard to have a celebration for us."

David looked contrite. "Aw, I'm sorry, Jen. I didn't mean right now. I thought maybe I could go later. Exercise Dynamo."

Jenny smiled halfheartedly. Despite herself she was a little hurt. "That's okay. Maybe later. I was thinking, though. Do you know any way we might be able to get some firewood? I thought we might have a fire this evening. Maybe toast some marshmallows."

Renee's eyes lit up. "That would be fun."

Fudge, Renee's puppy, ambled out into the kitchen, still limping slightly. He headed straight for Renee, who scooped him up with one hand while burying her nose in his fur. "Little chocolate ball," she told him. "I could just eat you up."

His little tail wagged furiously as his pink tongue snaked out to make contact with Renee's nose. It was hard to believe this was the same puppy they had found on the road that day. The pup had healed remarkably well in just three weeks, with only a slight limp testifying to his injury.

It had also been three weeks since Jenny had last seen Mitch except for quick glances at church, and then Amanda had been hanging on his arm. Jenny didn't know if he was angry at her for taking the pup and leaving, or not. All she did know for sure was that they seemed to always be at cross purposes. Jenny missed him, though she tried hard to keep him from her thoughts. He could never be a part of her life, so it was best to forget about him and get on with living.

"Jenny?"

She looked questioningly at David.

"I said there's an old paloverde about fifty feet from here. I could chop it up and bring the wood."

Jenny was reluctant. A twelve-year-old—no, he was thirteen now, wielding an ax? Was that a good idea? She had to let him grow up sometime, she supposed. Mitch had accused her of smothering David. She looked at him now, really looked, and realized that he was taller than she was now and his muscles were forming from the hard work he did helping Mitch. He was going to be as handsome as Renee was beautiful.

"Mitch has let me chop wood at his place," he told her, as though he could read her thoughts.

Irritation welled up inside that Mitch never considered it necessary to seek her permission. Still, David hadn't come to any harm under his tutelage. If anything he seemed to be blossoming into a responsible young man. She felt the annoyance drain out of her.

"Do we have an ax?" she questioned.

"Sure. There's one in the shed. There are a lot of tools in the shed. I've been cleaning them up the way Mitch showed me."

Figured. Smiling, Jenny reached out to ruffle his hair only to realize that to do so she would have to reach up.

"Go ahead," she told him.

"I'll help," Renee volunteered.

David fixed her with an eloquent look. "You can help carry the wood back, but I'll do the chopping. It's man's work."

Renee rolled her eyes but refrained from commenting as she traipsed along behind him.

Jenny watched them walk across the yard, thinking again how good life was. Renee was only slightly smaller than David, though David's gangliness was fast disappearing and turning into firm muscle. Renee was also starting to develop curves in all the right places. Jenny felt a slight qualm. What would the next few years bring? Both her siblings had the potential to become real heartbreakers. She only hoped she had the ability to channel them in the right direction.

Drying her hands on a paper towel, she got out the cake decorating paraphernalia.

Several hours later Jenny pulled into a parking spot at the Prescott National Forest picnic grounds. She had agreed to arrive a half hour later than everyone else to give the guests time to arrive. There were several cars, but the one that caught Jenny's attention was a blue Jeep. She should have realized that Hattie would have invited Mitch.

"Hey!" David exclaimed. "That looks like Mitch's Jeep."

"I wonder what he's doing here," Jenny said innocently.

As they approached the picnic tables, people jumped out from behind the trees surrounding the picnic area.

"Surprise!"

David stood with his mouth wide open, while Renee

ducked her head and turned a bright red. It only took David a moment before he was joining in the fun, friends from school slapping him on the back.

Several of Renee's friends had surrounded her, as well, and were hugging her and laughing.

"Well, at least they were surprised." Hattie laughed as she joined Jenny.

"You can say that again. It's been a while since I've seen David speechless."

Hattie pulled her arm through Jenny's and walked her toward the picnic tables.

"We thought we'd eat first and then have the twins open their presents."

"Sounds good to me," Jenny told her.

Jenny added her contribution to the potluck.

"This was a really good idea. I'm glad you thought of it."

Hattie grinned. "I'm a party person. I think I mentioned that before. Right now, we need to mingle."

If Hattie was a party person, Jenny was not. She had always hated large crowds, feeling self-conscious. She had never seemed to fit in. She liked people, but she preferred them in small quantities.

Hattie left her talking to Paul Taylor while Hattie wandered around speaking to others. Paul's eyes followed Hattie's progress a moment before he turned to Jenny. He smiled.

"She's one incredible woman. I've never known anyone so people-oriented."

Jenny nodded. "She's certainly that. I don't think there's anyone she wouldn't help."

Paul laughed. "I have to agree. If it hadn't been for her, I wouldn't be preacher here right now." At Jenny's look of inquiry he continued, "She knew my older sister. They went to school together when they were younger. When I graduated from seminary, Hattie heard that I was looking for a congregation. Since their previous preacher had just retired, she convinced the elders to offer me the position here. I'll be eternally grateful."

Glancing over her shoulder, Paul smiled. "Hi, Mitch. I thought I'd see you someplace around here."

Jenny felt her heart slam into her stomach and then kick into high speed. Schooling her features to mask her sudden nervousness, she turned and gave him a forced smile. "Hello, Mitch."

Mitch nodded to them both before addressing Paul. "Couldn't let my favorite partner down on his birthday."

Turning to Jenny, Mitch commented on David's new cowboy hat.

Jenny could see David across the way proudly strutting among his friends. She smiled. "He sure is proud of it."

"A birthday present, I take it?" Paul inquired.

"Yes. He's been after me for months now to get him one. I thought this was as good a time as any."

"Excuse me," Paul said. "I think Brother Johnson wants me." Nodding his head to both of them, he walked away.

Jenny didn't know whether to run or to stay. Feeling absurd for such foolishness, she looked up at Mitch.

"I'm glad you could come."

"I wouldn't have missed it for the world." He cocked his head slightly. "Surely you know that."

Jenny shrugged. Whatever his motives where she was concerned, it was hard to resist Mitch when he was being charming. She had to remind herself that he was here for David, not her.

"Would you like to look around?" he asked.

She hesitated, but could think of no real reason to refuse. If he could be congenial, so could she. "Sure."

Reaching out, Mitch took her hand and walked her away from the circle of people. The warmth of his fingers twined through hers left her feeling suddenly weak in the knees. She tried to pull her hand free, but he wouldn't release it. No matter how much she tried to distance herself from him and the feelings he engendered in her, she couldn't seem to do it.

He pointed out various landmarks, plants and trees, being careful to keep the conversation safely impersonal until Jenny finally relaxed. After about ten minutes he turned to her.

"We need to talk."

Jenny froze. Not now, she thought. She wasn't certain what he wanted to talk about, but she wasn't ready to discuss that potent kiss that had turned her neat little world upside down.

"What's wrong? Why have you been avoiding me?"

That was a very good question. How could she tell him that it was self-preservation on her part? Seeing Amanda had brought all of her insecurities to the fore again.

"I haven't been avoiding you…" she hedged.

"Is that the truth?"

She stared silently into his questioning eyes, the silence lengthening uncomfortably.

"That's what I thought."

"Tell me about Amanda," she said quickly and watched his face cloud over.

"What has Amanda to do with anything?"

"You were engaged once, weren't you?"

"I suppose Hattie told you that."

Jenny nodded, reaching out to pluck a leaf from a low-hanging branch. Twirling the stem in her fingers she asked, "Was there a reason she shouldn't have?"

Mitch let out a long sigh. "No. I suppose not. But that was a long time ago."

"Wasn't she at your barbecue a few weeks ago?" she asked, glancing sideways at him.

His chin lifted a notch. Turning to her, he pulled her to a stop. "Are you trying to hide behind her now, too?"

Jenny jerked away, her eyes sparking. "You're always

suggesting that I'm hiding behind someone. What do you consider that I need to hide from?"

"Your feelings, maybe?"

"I don't know what you're talking about."

"I think you do."

Her feelings? What about his? Could it be possible that she wasn't the only one caught up in this maelstrom of emotions? Their relationship had been like a never-ending roller-coaster ride. She wasn't about to admit to feelings for him unless he gave some indication of his own, and she didn't believe that was possible. What would a man like him possibly see in a woman like her? She found it positively ludicrous and it made her suspicious of his motives. She refused to be caught in a one-sided trap. Better to leave the words unsaid. She had the distinct feeling that once out in the open, her feelings could never be retracted.

"Don't be ridiculous. What feelings are you referring to, anyway?"

Taking her by the hand he pulled her to a stop again. His other hand captured her free hand. He gently tugged her closer and Jenny could feel her heart's increased rhythm when she saw the look in his eyes.

Jenny could only stare up at him, frustrated at the way he could reduce her to a mass of whirling confusion just by his mere touch. Regardless of her seesaw feelings about his reason for seeking her out, she couldn't bring herself to move. She wanted his kiss, but she couldn't bring herself to say so.

His lips covered hers in a kiss even more intoxicating than the first.

Letting go of her hands, he wrapped his arms around her. As she had felt before, so she felt now. Safe. Cherished. Protected. Her hands slid up his arms before gently wrapping around his neck. It seemed an eternity before

Mitch finally pulled his lips away and stared down into her eyes.

"Those feelings," he told her huskily.

Jenny called herself all kinds of a fool as she realized that she had fallen irrevocably in love with Mitch, and she was too dazed to think clearly about what she should do about it.

"Jenny? Mitch? I thought I saw them come this way."

By the time David and Mark reached them they were standing a safe distance apart.

"There you are. We've been looking all over for you," David complained.

"Well, now you've found us," Mitch told him reasonably. Jenny couldn't have spoken if she had wanted to.

"Mom wants to eat now," Mark told them.

Once again curling his fingers around Jenny's hand, they followed the boys back to the clearing. For the time being, they seemed to have reached a pax in their turbulent relationship. For the rest of the day Jenny lived in a kind of dreamworld.

Mitch remained by Jenny's side for most of the day. They sat together to eat. He was there when David and Renee opened their presents. When they reached Young's Farm, he helped them choose a pumpkin from the hundreds in the field and then cheerfully paid for it. Sitting on the sweet-smelling haystacks, they rode in the tractor-pulled wagon back to the main buildings.

After they toured the facilities Mitch bought them a fresh baked pie from the cafeteria. They argued good-naturedly over the type, but finally compromised on apple.

"It doesn't make sense to buy a pumpkin pie when you have the pumpkin to make your own," Jenny remonstrated with the twins.

The twins wandered off to watch the singing sideshow while Mitch took Jenny to the country store. The tiny little room was filled to capacity with both items and people.

As they were walking out the door, Jenny noticed some of the crafts for sale. The prices seemed exorbitant to her, but Annie wouldn't have agreed.

"Jenny!"

It was as though her thoughts had conjured the young woman up.

"Annie. What are you doing here?"

"I always come to the pumpkin festival. It's tradition. Besides, I have to keep an eye on the competition." She grinned, pointing at the craft display. Looking over Jenny's shoulder, she smiled at Mitch.

"Long time, no see, cowboy."

Mitch grinned at her. "Not my fault. You're the one who moved to the big city, far away from your friends."

Annie made a rude sound with her lips. "I'd hardly call it an insurmountable distance. Speaking of which…" She turned to Jenny again. "Have you thought about what I said? About moving to Prescott?"

This was not something Jenny particularly wanted to discuss right now, but knowing Annie as she did, unless she gave her an answer she would be nagged to death.

"I've thought about it, yes."

"Well, have you talked with the twins?"

"Not yet." She turned to face Mitch and was surprised at the absolute immobility of his features. They seemed to be carved in granite and his eyes had taken on an icy hue.

"If you'll excuse me, I need to talk to someone," he said and, pushing past Jenny, went swiftly out the door.

"Now, what was that all about?" Annie wondered, frowning at Mitch's retreating figure.

Jenny shook her head. She was back on that roller coaster again. How could a man be so fun and considerate one minute and as cold as ice the next? She was thankful that she had restrained the impulse to tell Mitch how she really felt about him. At least she had salvaged her pride. Funny thing about pride, though; it was a very lonely feeling.

Chapter 9

Jenny pulled the pumpkin pies from the oven, sniffing appreciatively before setting them on the hot pads on the counter.

This was the last of the pumpkin from the one Mitch had bought almost four weeks ago now. She had taken it home, baked it and then scooped out the flesh and frozen it. Out of her efforts she had managed to get several bags of pumpkin to freeze.

The twins had enjoyed the fruits of her labor: pumpkin bread, pumpkin muffins, pumpkin pies. And every time she made something, remembrances of that day came back to haunt her. Mitch holding her hand… Mitch smiling and picking pieces of hay from her hair, then tickling her nose with it… Mitch smiling that warm smile that sent her senses soaring…

It hadn't taken long to realize what had brought about Mitch's changed attitude. He believed that she, like Amanda and his mother, was longing for city life. Jenny smiled wryly. If only he knew. But Jenny had decided that if something was developing between her and Mitch—and she still had a hard time believing that—it was something best left alone.

Until Mitch could bring himself to let go of the past, for them there could be no future. He would always be watching. Wondering if the woman he loved would leave him again. And how exactly did Amanda fit into all of this?

It occurred to Jenny that she had always had insecurities of her own because of her looks. To see someone so handsome, wealthy and charming with such vulnerabilities was enlightening.

Turning from her perusal of the landscape outside the kitchen window, her look returned to the pies cooling on the counter. They'd been invited to Hattie's for Thanksgiving tomorrow. Jenny wrinkled her nose at the thought that she had almost cried off of going because Mitch would be there. The twins would have been devastated.

She had talked with the twins about moving to Prescott. As she had figured, they both had adamantly refused, although David was by far the most vociferous. His attitude had taken a one-hundred-eighty-degree turnaround. In a way it was a relief. In another part of her mind, she still questioned the wisdom of allowing the twins to grow up in such isolation.

Still, rather than being harmful, the opposite seemed to be the case. They were becoming more mature. Less selfish. Of course much of this was due to their growing spirituality, and as long as she lived she would be thankful to Hattie Ames for pressuring her into going to church.

The problems Jenny had to face no longer seemed insurmountable when she had someone so powerful to lean on. God's love was continually made manifest in the very things He continued to do for her.

Fudge's joyous yapping brought her to a realization of the time. The twins must be home from school.

David breezed through the door first, flinging his books on the coffee table. "Four days off!"

Jenny grinned as Renee followed her brother at a more sedate pace.

"You make it sound like a reprieve from jail," Jenny told him.

"Isn't it?" he quipped. "Man! It's flat cold out there!"

"Still, it's not as bad as New York," Renee told him as she ruffled Fudge in her arms. There was no hint of the dog's injury anymore and he was growing like a weed. He was Renee's constant companion, rarely letting her out of his sight when she was home.

Jenny had to agree about the weather. After the long, hot summer she was unprepared for the cold of a winter in the desert. As Renee said, it was nothing like New York, but still cold enough to almost freeze water at night.

She had spent the past month hurriedly putting together a couple of quilt tops. The designs were her own and reflected the tastes of each twin, but finding time to quilt them was a problem. She had started quilting David's last night, staying up long into the night. Since she and Renee shared a bed, David was in greater need of the warm blanket.

The cold was beginning to worry Jenny. If it was this cold now, how cold would it get in December and January? Supposedly they were the coldest months.

It still amazed her that Cousin Tito had refused to add heating and air-conditioning to the cabin. Her vivid imagination pictured him huddled by the fire, staring into the crackling flames with his hands wrapped around a hot drink. Had he been lonely here? She wished she knew more about the man who had been so generous with her family.

David interrupted her thoughts. "Mitch is taking me out later to chop wood. He owns land in Prescott and gets his wood from there. Is it okay?"

"Since you're telling me you're going, I assume you have already made plans. Now's a fine time to ask permission."

"He just asked today," David replied defensively. "He stopped the school bus to ask. Said if it wasn't convenient I could give him a call and let him know."

There was really no reason to refuse. She should be grateful.

"I guess it's okay. We definitely need the wood."

"That's what I thought."

Sniffing the air, David turned an appreciative look on his sister. "You made pumpkin pies."

"Yes, and you stay out of them. They're for tomorrow."

"Aww…"

"And take your books to your room."

David headed into his room, dragging his things along with him.

"David?"

"Yeah?"

"Is Mitch stopping by here to pick you up, or do I need to take you to his place?" Jenny crossed her fingers.

"He said he'll pick me up here since it's on his way to Prescott," he answered, peeking his head back around the corner of the door. "Why? You wantin' to hide out again?"

"David!"

David looked at his twin. "What? It's the truth. She's always hiding out. Especially from Mitch."

Is that how David really saw her? It made her sound like some kind of slinking mouse. Remembering Mitch's comparison, she had to admit they were probably right. She had always been an introvert, even in college. But her desire to avoid Mitch had nothing whatsoever to do with that.

Deciding to ignore his comment, she told David, "Dress warmly, and don't forget your gloves."

She turned and retreated to the warmth of the kitchen. She leaned against the sink and stared out at the autumn landscape. So, the twins had not been fooled. Giving herself a mental shake, she reached into the cupboard and pulled out a pot. Hot cocoa sounded good. Maybe she would put some in a thermos and send it with David.

Ten minutes later she set three steaming mugs of cocoa on a tray and plopped a large marshmallow into each one. Taking the tray to the living room she set it on the coffee table in front of Renee, who was busily working on her homework.

"You have four days, you know," Jenny told her.

She put her books aside. "I know. I just thought it would be better to get it out of the way and not worry about it all weekend."

"Well, that's true enough."

David came in from the other room. "Do you want me to stack some more wood for the fire?" he asked, tucking in his green flannel shirt.

"That would be great. When is Mitch coming for you?"

David picked up his mug, taking a large draft. His blue eyes widened in surprise, filling with sudden tears. Jenny watched in amusement as he rolled the drink around in his mouth trying to cool it enough to swallow. Finally he was able to gulp it down.

"Yeow! Why don't you warn a guy?"

Jenny shook her head and grinned.

Renee gave him a scathing look. "Anyone who can't tell a drink is hot by the steam curling into the air must be dense. I think you need to leave off the Stetson for a while and let your brain air out."

David scowled. "Oh, yeah? Well, what about—"

Jenny interrupted him. "You didn't answer my question."

"When's Mitch coming? He said he'd come by about two. Said it would still be daylight for a while, since we only had a half day of school."

Jenny retraced her steps to the kitchen. "Good. That will give you time to eat something."

David followed her. "Mmm. Something sure smells good. Is it soup?"

"Yes. You and Renee get yourselves washed up."

After they had all eaten, they once again gathered around the fireplace. Except for the kitchen when she baked, the living room was the only really warm room in the cabin. Still, the cabin was very weathertight and if they left the bedroom doors open the fire took the chill off. All in all, it was rather cozy. Jenny decided she must be from pioneer stock, because she found it invigorating.

It wasn't long until they heard an approaching vehicle.

David jumped up and ran for his bedroom. "That must be Mitch. I'll get my coat."

Renee glanced up at Jenny speculatively, but Jenny ignored her.

"I suppose I should invite him in," she told Renee without moving, ringing her hands around her mug.

Renee continued to stare at her, her lips twitching. "Mmm."

Jenny threw her a disgusted look before striding to the door. She opened the door just as the Jeep rolled to a stop. Mitch didn't bother to get out; he merely rolled down his window. If it was cold outside, it was nothing compared to the ice in those green eyes.

"David ready?" he asked as she came down the steps.

"Almost."

She looked everywhere but at that granite face. "Would you like to come in?"

"No. We don't have time. Darkness falls early this time of year."

"So I noticed."

What an absurd conversation between two people who once had shared such a beautiful, intimate moment. Was Mitch remembering, too? If he was, he was keeping it well hidden.

Before she could form another coherent thought David pushed by her. "Hi."

"Hi, yourself," Mitch answered. "Got your ax?"

"I'll get it."

Jenny watched him go around the corner of the house. When she turned back she was startled by the look on Mitch's face. It was there only an instant, but it caused her errant heart to start thudding heavily. The tenderness she thought she saw was more than likely only wishful thinking on her part.

Both remained silently watching the corner where David had disappeared. Before long he returned, the ax thrown over his shoulder.

"Be careful," Jenny told him as he climbed in beside Mitch. He rolled his eyes.

"Don't worry. I'll take good care of him," Mitch reassured her.

"I never worry when he's with you," she told him softly. His glance flicked swiftly to her face. He stared at her a long moment before he started the engine.

"We should be back by six but if we're not, don't worry. I thought we might stop for a meal, if that's okay with you."

"Sure."

He put the car into gear and was about to drive forward when she remembered the cocoa she had prepared for them.

"Wait!"

Running into the kitchen she returned with the thermos and two old mugs.

"Something to keep you warm," she told them, handing the thermos through the window to Mitch. Her hand touched his briefly and the jolt she felt had nothing to do with static electricity. She raised startled eyes to his and found him watching her intently, his eyes dilating until they were more black than green. He looked as if he was about to speak but then decided not to.

Stepping away from the car she told him in a voice that shook, "I'll see you later."

Nodding, he drove away without once looking back.

"Could you put the pies on that table over there with the other desserts?"

Hattie was rushing from one area to another trying to see that everything was being accomplished according to her plan.

"What can I do?" Jenny asked.

"Let's see…" Pausing, Hattie looked around her. "It looks as though everything is under control."

"Mom! The gravy is ruined!" April wailed, coming from the kitchen.

"What! What happened?" Taking her daughter by the arm, Hattie marched her back to the kitchen, Jenny following. Smoke was billowing from the frying pan on the stove, where a blob of black liquid resided.

Jenny grabbed an oven mitt and pulled the pan from the stove while Hattie hurried over and threw open the patio door that led into the kitchen.

April looked so woebegone that Jenny was instantly sorry for her.

"The phone rang," she told them sorrowfully.

Hattie stared belligerently at her oldest child. "Let me guess. Dennis."

"We only talked a few minutes," April protested.

Jenny laid a hand on Hattie's arm. "Why don't you let me make another batch of gravy?"

"I didn't invite you here to work," Hattie protested, giving her daughter an eloquent look.

"I know, but I'd like to. It would make me feel more comfortable."

"Well…if you're sure. Everything you need should be right over there."

She pointed to the counter where a conglomeration of

kitchen paraphernalia was strewed across its surface. Flour was scattered here and there, on the floor as well as the cabinets. Hattie turned to Jenny. They stared at each other several seconds before they broke into spontaneous laughter.

"You go take care of your guests. I'll take care of the gravy and the mess," Jenny told her, pushing Hattie toward the doorway.

"Okay. As long as you don't hide yourself out here too long."

Jenny watched Hattie's retreating back before turning to the work at hand. "Everyone thinks I'm hiding out," she muttered, reaching for the flour. She cleared a place on the counter and dumped the contents of the burned gravy down the garbage disposal.

"Hattie sent me in to see if you needed any help." Mitch's deep voice made her jump and she dropped the whisk, rescuing it before it hit the floor.

"Uh...no. Not that I know of." One look at his face and she knew he would rather be anywhere right now besides standing in this doorway. She sighed soundlessly, regretting the fact that they seemed to be back to square one in their relationship. His steady stare made her nervous.

"I just have to make some gravy. Seems April got tied up on the phone and burned it, so I volunteered to make some more. The kitchen's a real mess, but that's what happens when you're serving a large meal to a large crowd." Jenny started clearing a space as she continued to nervously prattle on. "It's amazing how cold the weather has gotten. I appreciate you taking David for the firewood. I—"

"Slow down!" he interrupted. "Shift your tongue into neutral a minute."

He was leaning against the doorjamb and grinning at her.

The flush on her cheeks was not only due to the warm kitchen. Her eyes flashed, but she forced herself to hold her tongue. She reached for the cornstarch, giving herself time to stifle the urge to fling the whole sorry mess in his face.

* * *

Mitch didn't miss the fire in her eyes, nor the ramrod-straight set of her shoulders. He'd ticked her off again, and no wonder with a comment such as that. There were times he wanted to shake her. Instead he usually wound up saying something he shouldn't, but he couldn't seem to help himself. What had started off as a promising friendship had turned into something much more and now he was having a hard time forgetting the past few months and finding that earlier footing.

After several minutes of cold silence it became obvious that Jenny wasn't going to say anything more. He supposed he deserved it. He exhaled through the side of his mouth.

"I'm sorry. That was rude."

Jenny remained silent, measuring the cornstarch into the turkey drippings. She began whipping it with unnecessary force, giving vent to her aggravation.

Her bottom lip was protruding in a childish pout as she poured the mixture into the saucepan. Mitch grinned again. He should really try to focus his eyes somewhere besides those rosebud lips. They reminded him of things best forgotten if he wanted to keep his peace of mind.

His anger was directed more at himself than her, anyway. She had every right to live in Prescott if she chose. She had the twins to think of. It was his own fault for allowing himself to care so much.

"I really am sorry," he told her softly.

Her shoulders slumped. He couldn't begin to interpret the look that flitted across her face and then was gone. She threw him a halfhearted smile over her shoulder.

"I'm sorry. I guess I was just concentrating too hard on getting this gravy right. You have nothing to apologize for."

That was Jenny, always the peacemaker. Straightening, he walked over and stood beside her and saw her tense, increasing his frustration with the whole situation. He frowned, stifling the urge to whip her around and kiss the living daylights out of her.

"How do you get it not to have lumps?" he asked, accepting the olive branch she was offering.

Sighing, Jenny continued stirring the gravy.

"Technique."

When it was time to eat, Hattie reached for a spoon and clinked it against her glass.

"Okay, everyone. We have a tradition at the Ameses' house," she announced. "When we thank the Lord for the food, everyone prays. You don't have to say much, just one thing you're grateful for. It has to be something personal. Not things in general, such as health or wealth. And not Jesus because, after all, we're all thankful for that. Jacob will start and we'll go clockwise around the table until I finish. Okay?"

Jenny wasn't too sure about praying in front of people. Prayer was a private thing for her. Something between God and her. Nevertheless, she decided to enter into the spirit of the thing. Pushing her reservations aside, she wondered what she was most thankful for. God had done so much for her lately. Given her so much.

She listened as one after another added their thanks to the prayer chain. A knot formed in her throat when Renee thanked God for Jenny and her little dog, Fudge. What a blessing to have such a sweet, loving sister. Her heart almost melted when David added his thanks for a sister who loved him enough to make sacrifices for him. He added his thanks for Mitch, who taught him a lot. Jenny desperately blinked back the tears trying to force their way out.

Annie thanked the Lord for her fiancé, Jeremy. Opening her eyes briefly Jenny watched Jeremy squeeze Annie's hand and gaze lovingly at her. Jenny hurriedly closed her eyes again.

When it came to Jenny's turn, she suddenly knew what she would say. What she was most thankful for.

"Father, although it's sometimes hard to understand or accept the things that happen to us, thank You for allowing circumstances to work to bring me to live in Mayer. Without Your leading, I would not have found You again."

It was only as everyone was serving themselves that Jenny realized she had missed Mitch's prayer. She must have been so caught up in her thoughts that she hadn't heard him. Frowning in frustration, she decided to ask Renee later.

The rest of the evening seemed to go better after Jenny and Mitch's talk in the kitchen. Mitch forgot to hold himself aloof and became the charming man Jenny knew he was capable of being. For a time, she was able to relax and enjoy herself. As she had promised herself earlier, she decided to let go and just have fun. And surprisingly, she did.

Afterward, everyone sat around grumbling about their overindulgence at the dinner table. Despite protests, everyone knew that later there would be room for dessert. In the meantime, conversation seemed the only thing anyone had enough energy to contemplate. Everyone except David.

"I'm ready to play Ping-Pong," David addressed Mark.

Mark groaned. Picking up a pillow, he threw it at David.

"You've got to be kidding."

"Aw, come on," David urged him. "If you don't, you won't have room for dessert. And Jenny makes the best pumpkin pie around."

"In that case, I guess I need to make some room, too." Mitch pulled himself to his feet. Putting an arm around David's shoulders, they ambled toward the door to the den. Mark slowly rose to his feet and followed them out.

Hattie watched them go with a look of disbelief on her face. "I can't even move, let alone think about dessert."

Getting up himself, Jacob grinned down at her. Bending, he kissed her lightly on the lips. "That's okay. We men will work off some of our dinner. And have no fear, those pies will be consumed."

Hattie smacked his leg as he went by. "Gluttony is a sin, you know."

Jenny watched their exchange with frank envy. More and more, Jenny longed for such a marriage herself. Was that something God had planned for her or was she destined to spend her life alone? Whatever happened, she must trust the Lord to do what was best for her.

Mitch stepped to Hattie's side and together they watched Jenny's car disappear around the corner. Hattie looked up at him, the laughter of moments before erased from her face.

"You're a stubborn, pigheaded mule. You're going to lose the best thing that's ever happened to you because of your stupid pride."

His nostrils flared slightly. "It's my business," he told her coldly, turning to go back inside.

Hattie grabbed the sleeve of his sweater. "Oh, no, you don't. You're not getting off that easily."

Mitch glanced down at the hand curled into the fabric of his sweater. Raising one eyebrow, he told her softly, "Mind your own business, Hattie."

He couldn't be upset with Hattie's blunt assessment. They had been through too much together for him to find offense with her interfering. She would say whatever she had to say and hang the consequences.

"Do you remember when Jacob asked me to marry him?"

He knew where this was going. That had been a turbulent time for all of them. "That was different."

"Was it? Was it really, Mitch? Tell me how?"

Mitch snorted. "It was obvious that you loved each other. Someone had to do something. You're both so pigheaded, neither of you would listen to reason."

She watched his face closely. "You still haven't told me how it was different."

Mitch looked away from her. "Are you trying to say

that Jenny and I are in love with each other or that we're both pigheaded?"

"I didn't say anything. I merely asked a question."

Blowing out his breath harshly, Mitch raked his hand through his hair in frustration. "She wants to move to Prescott."

"Who told you that?" Hattie asked him. She wrapped her arms around her waist. He sighed with frustration. If she wasn't going to give up on the conversation, then he had best be the gentleman his father had taught him to be. He pulled off his sweater and wrapped it around her.

"I heard her and Annie talking."

Hattie nodded her head. "And Jenny said she wanted to move?"

Mitch looked at her perplexed. "That's what I heard."

"Are you sure you didn't hear Annie asking Jenny to think about it?"

"Same thing."

"It's not the same thing at all."

Leaning his hands against the veranda rail Mitch gazed up at the stars. "She'll go. Sooner or later. They always do."

"I haven't," she told him softly.

Flicking her a glance, he smiled without mirth. "You're different."

"So is Jenny."

Mitch snorted, turning back to study the stars. "I had started to think so, now I'm not so sure."

"Is that why you're using Amanda as a shield?"

He glared at her, but she glared back at him undaunted. "The problem is within you, Mitch," she told him. "You have to forget the past. Forgive the hurts. Until you do, you will never be truly happy." Reaching out, she gently massaged his shoulders. "Jenny had her own fears to conquer and she's done that remarkably well. Now you have to face yours."

Long minutes ticked by before he answered and then his voice was little more than a tortured whisper.

"I can't."

"I've never known you to be a coward."

Anger flamed through him and as quickly died. She was right and he knew it, despite his reluctance to admit it. He *was* being a coward about jumping wholeheartedly into a relationship again. He was playing with fire where Jenny was concerned. One of them was bound to get hurt, and he didn't want it to be him, but then again, he didn't want it to be her, either. The best thing he could do for both of them was just to leave things as they were.

Hattie patted his arm. "I'll pray for you." She handed him his sweater, turned and went back inside the house, leaving him alone with his morose thoughts.

Chapter 10

The next several weeks passed in a blur of activity. With the Christmas season being so near, Jenny had more orders than she could possibly fill. Her most popular item seemed to be the quilted wall hangings she made of desert scenes. Using soft browns, pale turquoises, deep melons and rich ambers, she created swirling, shifting patterns of incredible beauty.

The trouble was that she didn't have enough hours in the day to get everything accomplished that she wanted to do. Annie was continually calling her with new orders that customers hoped to have in time for Christmas. Added to that was her desire to get something extra special for the twins this holiday season. For the past several years they had struggled in poverty. Now she wanted to make it up to them.

Income from the craft shop had increased dramatically, but Jenny was uncertain just how long that would last. It was possible that orders might dry up after Christmas was over.

In the meantime she had been busily engaged in trying to create the perfect Christmas for them all. Although Hattie had extracted a promise from her to spend a portion of Christmas with the Ameses, Jenny wanted a Christmas of her own, complete with decorations, baking and all the regular holiday entrapments.

Pulling a fruitcake from the oven, Jenny chuckled. It seemed she spent more time in the kitchen than any other area of the house. Of course the fact that it was also the warmest might have had something to do with it.

She lifted the cake to her nose, sniffing deeply. Most people didn't like fruitcake, although from what she could tell at the stores, someone must be buying it. They seemed to fill shelves wherever she went.

She placed the cake on a rack to cool for ten minutes before turning it out of the pan. The recipe was one she had concocted during a cooking class in college. She had won praise from the teachers and students alike.

After turning the cake out onto its side, Jenny plopped down on a kitchen chair. Reaching across the table, she lifted a sugar cookie from the platter waiting to be iced. She nibbled the cookie, mentally checking off her to-do list.

The fruitcake was the last of the baking for today. Unconsciously she sighed. She had been keeping herself busy trying to ward off thoughts that were becoming all too frequent. It wasn't working. Mental images of Mitch wove their way in and out with each project she attempted. Making a wall hanging, she would wonder about the inside of Mitch's house. Would a particular wall hanging look good hanging above his fireplace? She knew he had one since he and David often went to chop more wood.

When she was baking, she would imagine what it would be like to cook for him. To be married to him. At this point she would usually jump up and rush to the next task, running from her futile daydreams. Trying to get the man out of her mind was proving a lot less fruitful than the fruit-cake she had just made.

She and Mitch had avoided each other as much as possible the past several weeks. At times she would catch him staring at her with an intense, enigmatic expression. When she caught his eye, he would quickly turn away. These occasions always left her flustered.

As usual when thoughts of Mitch got too intense, Jenny shifted gears. Dreaming seemed so useless an occupation.

Jenny inventoried the kitchen table. Fresh chocolate-chip cookies nestled in the center of a table almost groaning under the weight of the goodies weighing it down. She had kept herself busy, yes, but what good had it done her?

She wandered out to the living room, smiling when she noticed Fudge curled up on the rug close to the front door. No matter how cold it might get, he would not leave his guard position until Renee arrived. Jenny had tried to coax him close to the fire. She had even gone so far as to fix a blanket there and put the pup on it. He had looked at her with sad, perplexed eyes and from then on she hadn't the heart to try it again.

On the other hand, Jenny was thankful for the warmth of the fire. Curling up on the sofa in her favorite spot, she reached for the wall hanging she was presently working on. She smoothed a hand across the material, marveling at the blend of colors and textures. She wouldn't have believed it possible that these particular colors and materials would work so well together.

Although the woven wall hangings were less complicated to make and took less time, she much preferred the ones she quilted.

This specific one was a Christmas creation requested by one of Annie's favorite clients. Dark navy blue silk shimmered as the sky with rhinestone sequins glittering in diamondlike brilliance as the stars. Soft velour curved gracefully across the bottom in various shades of gray and black, making it a picture of nighttime tranquility. Rough seersucker fabric gave texture to the adobe buildings of long-ago Bethlehem. One brilliant yellow satin star slanted its rays across the nighttime sky, lighting a path to a small cave nestled in the hills.

The wall hanging reminded her just what this season was about. Although no one knew for certain just what time of year Christ was born, the birth of Christ was the start of God's wonderful plan for mankind's redemption and worthy of celebration at any time.

But it was His death on the cross that made that salvation possible. She had shed many tears while working on this project, knowing that even if she had been the only person on earth, He would have died for her. Perhaps it was all that meditation that had made this one of the most beautiful pieces she had ever created. Every stitch was made with love.

The hanging had turned out much better than she had anticipated. There was a certain free license to combine unusual materials when it came to wall hangings. Annie would be pleased.

As Jenny reluctantly set the last stitches in place, Fudge lifted his head, his brown, fuzzy ears cocked forward. Glancing at the anniversary clock on the mantel, Jenny smiled. Right on time.

It was only moments before Jenny could hear the familiar footfalls on the porch. As usual, David was the first through the door.

Jenny got to her feet, ready to go through the daily ritual of reminding her brother to put his things away.

"Guess what?" he said before he even had time to take off his coat. "Mitch's mother is here."

Jenny looked startled, glancing behind him. "Here?"

"No," he told her impatiently. "I mean here in town."

Jenny stood statue-still, blinking at her brother. Her

mind had gone blank at David's declaration. "I thought she was dead," she whispered.

"So did we," Renee agreed, coming in and scooping up her beloved buddy.

"I can't believe it." Jenny moved to the fireplace, staring somberly into the flickering flames of the fire. Searing images danced in front of her eyes. "How did you find this out?"

"Mark told us at school," David answered, pulling off his coat and dropping it on a chair. "Said she's staying with the Ameses for right now."

"Not with Mitch?"

"Nope."

Had Mitch refused to let his own mother stay with him? She could well understand it if that was the case. Although she didn't know the whole story, she knew enough to understand that a boy of ten might have been so hurt that he was a bitter, unforgiving man at thirty-three. Having had a mother who was devoted to her children, Jenny was hard-pressed to understand someone who could desert her own child.

"Mmm. I smell something good," Renee commented. "I love coming home and knowing that you'll be here, Jen. And you always have a snack for us."

Jenny watched Renee head for the kitchen, a sudden lump forming in her throat. She could never have hoped for a better compliment than that.

David finished taking off his boots and putting on his slippers that perpetually sat beside the fire. "Yep. Makes you feel kinda…I don't know. It just makes you feel good."

Without even looking Jenny's way he followed his sister into the kitchen. Sudden tears came to Jenny's eyes and she swallowed the reminder of where to put his coat. The twins rarely paid her compliments, but this had to be one of the nicest.

Later, after supper, Renee took her books and curled

up by the fire. David decided to help Jenny in the kitchen, which caused her to look at him sharply.

"Are you feeling all right?" she asked suspiciously.

"Sure." He continued drying a plate before stacking it in the cupboard. He was working so industriously that Jenny became even more suspicious.

Placing her hands on her hips, she decided to confront him outright. "Okay. Out with it."

"Out with what?" he asked, giving her his most angelic look.

That look always portended trouble. She didn't know who he was trying to fool, but it certainly wasn't her. She frowned at him. "David, I know you better than you know yourself. You might as well just come out with it. What do you want?"

"Jiminy Crickets! Can't a guy even give a helping hand around here without someone questioning his motives?"

"David."

He looked into her eyes briefly before quickly turning away. Pulling another plate from the stack, he began to methodically dry it. Jenny waited a moment before reaching out and taking it away from him. She set both towel and plate on the counter then pointed to the table.

"Sit," she commanded.

Reluctantly, David sat. Refusing to look at Jenny, he pulled a cookie from the top stack of chocolate chips. Jenny was really becoming alarmed now.

Sliding into the seat across from him, she reached across and took the cookie from his hand. She didn't want him to have any excuse not to talk.

"What is it, David?" she asked softly. "Are you in trouble in school?"

He looked at her in surprise. "No way!"

"Then what is it?" she demanded, her irritation growing.

He looked down at the table, drawing circles with his fingers. "I just wondered if you might do me a favor."

That's what this was all about? "Well, for crying out loud. Why didn't you just say so? What do you want me to do?"

"Actually," he mumbled, "it's for someone else."

Jenny studied his downbent head. Whatever it was, he was having a hard time trying to tell her.

"Okay. What do you want me to do? And for whom?"

David remained silent for several more minutes. Jenny had to rein in her impatience.

"Mitch's housekeeper had to go back east for a while and he's without someone to clean for him and he doesn't have someone to cook for him and I told him you would be willing to help," he finally blurted without taking a breath.

Jenny felt the color drain from her face. She opened and closed her mouth several times, the words sticking in her throat.

"You told him what?" she managed to croak out. "David! You know I'm so busy right now I don't even have enough time to finish all the things I need to get done. How could you?"

He stared at her sullenly. "You're always talking about wanting to help other people like Hattie does all the time. I just thought since we lived so close and all, that we could help Mitch."

"We?" she asked him. *"We?"* Her voice rose at least three octaves.

"Yeah. I can help, too. Renee's already said she'll take over the cleaning of the cabin. We'll be out of school next week, anyway. Besides," he added as inducement, "he says he'll pay you."

"David Allen Gordon!"

David flinched. "Okay, so I shoulda asked first, but Mitch'll be here any minute to talk to you about it."

Jenny's eyes widened in horror. She opened her mouth to remonstrate with him, but she could think of nothing to say that wouldn't be scathing. Instead, snapping her mouth closed, she whirled around and stalked out of the room.

Jenny watched the blue Jeep approaching with a feeling of déjà vu. Her heart started pounding the minute she saw his vehicle turn onto their track. Shivering, she pulled her crocheted shawl closer around her. Right now she could have cheerfully strangled her brother.

What was Mitch thinking now? Since she had had so little forewarning, she had no idea what she was going to say to him. Somehow she had to politely tell him that she couldn't do what David had suggested. She didn't have the time. And that wasn't just a meager excuse, either. She was already so bogged down with work; she couldn't possibly fit in anything else.

Mitch climbed out of the Jeep and studied her slowly before finally meeting her on the porch.

"Jenny." He nodded, his voice nothing more than polite.

"Mitch." She returned his greeting.

"You'll catch your death of cold out here in that," he told her, indicating her shawl.

She smiled. She had intended to mull over her choice of words in the privacy of the porch, but there hadn't been enough time. There was nothing else to do but invite him in. They sure couldn't stand out here in the biting cold. She held open the door and he motioned for her to precede him.

One corner of Mitch's mouth curved upward slightly when he saw David rapidly disappear through his bedroom door. It should have occurred to him that Jenny hadn't made the offer David had suggested, but just now he didn't seem to be thinking too straight. He couldn't blame her. He hadn't been exactly friendly lately, trying to distance himself from a relationship that was fast getting out of hand. At least on his part.

He smiled at Renee, who smiled warmly back. No problem there, he decided. This whole thing had probably been David's doing.

"Hi, Renee."

"Hi." She uncurled herself from her cramped position, stretching widely. She smiled down at Fudge, who was whimpering softly.

"Okay, okay," she told him. "I'll take you out for a while."

The pup seemed to know exactly what she said, because he flew to the door, his tail wagging in his excitement. Mitch grinned.

"Don't you let him out by himself?"

"Not yet. He's still too little. I'm afraid he might get hurt by a coyote or something."

"I see." Mitch watched her pull on her coat while the dog patiently waited at her feet.

Jenny motioned to a chair and sat across from him, her glance straying to Renee, as well. They both waited until she disappeared out the door before turning their eyes toward each other. A second later they heard the kitchen door slam shut. Laughter danced in Mitch's eyes.

"I take it that was David."

Jenny grimaced. "Probably. The little monster."

The smile reached all the way to his mouth. "I assume you knew nothing about the suggestion to be my housekeeper for a while."

She shook her head. "I didn't."

He leaned back against the chair, raking both hands through his hair. He slowly released a breath. "I suppose I should have figured that. I seem to be a little slow in the brain department these days."

He looked utterly confused, and Jenny's heart reached out to him.

"I'm sorry—"

"It's just that I'm a little desperate right now," he interrupted. "It's a bad time for my housekeeper to be leaving, but her daughter is having a baby and she wants to be there. My mother has suddenly appeared and she was hoping to camp out at the ranch. From what I can remember, she wouldn't be much good in the homemaking department."

Jenny could hear the bitterness in his voice, but there was an air of excited expectancy, as well.

"Have you seen her yet?"

"No." The answer was short and clipped, precluding further discussion on the subject.

"I'd like to help, Mitch, but I'm really busy." She gestured to the wall hanging she had just finished that day. "I have more than I can handle right now."

"I understand. I guess I was just a little desperate. I should have realized. Hattie told me how busy you were."

Jenny studied her fingernails silently. Mitch sounded lost, unsure of what to do. It was so unlike him, it truly concerned her. He was uncomfortable asking for her help, she could tell that. But that's not what made him so hesitant. He really didn't know what to do with his own mother, who had suddenly showed up on his doorstep after twenty-three years. Impulsively, Jenny made a totally illogical decision. She looked at him sitting there with his hands pulled back through his hair, his eyes closed.

"Actually, I'm pretty much finished with my Christmas baking and I'm somewhat caught up on my crafting. I think I could help you a few hours a week, if that would work?"

His eyes flew open and he stared at her silently for several long seconds.

"I couldn't ask you to do that. As you said, you have enough to do."

His lips said one thing but his eyes pleaded in a way she hadn't the heart to refuse.

"Let's see," she said, ignoring his rebuttal. "I could come tomorrow at about nine o'clock and stay till about two. That would still give me time to fix something for the twins and be here when they get home."

Mitch protested again, but there was very little heart to it.

"How long do you think she'll stay?" Jenny asked, and could have immediately bitten off her tongue at the look on his face.

"I doubt if she'll stay long. Probably just long enough to tell me what she wants," he answered darkly.

Jenny merely nodded. "If you have all the supplies, I can fix a meal for you and your mother before I leave. That way she would be able to stay with you as of tomorrow."

He looked relieved and hopeful at the same time. "Will you stay long enough to meet her?"

She could see in his eyes the answer he wanted her to give.

"Sure. As long as you have her there by two o'clock."

"Great! I'll make the arrangements." He got quickly to his feet, probably anxious to leave before she could change her mind.

He went to the door and opened it. Leaning out, he searched the area around him. "You guys can come out of hiding now. I'm leaving."

David popped around the corner, grinning sheepishly. Renee followed, with Fudge bringing up the rear.

Jenny joined the twins on the porch and watched while Mitch buckled his seat belt. He winked at David before turning to her.

"I'll see you tomorrow, then. Nine o'clock."

Jenny nodded, refusing to look at either of her siblings.

It was only as she was preparing for bed that night that she began to have doubts. Large, nagging ones.

Chapter 11

Standing back to survey the table she had just set, Jenny gave a satisfied nod. Everything was as it should be. Reaching her hands behind her neck, she started massaging out the kinks. She was tired already, but she still had a long day ahead of her.

She went swiftly from room to room to assure herself that everything was in apple-pie order. Since Mitch's housekeeper had only been gone a week, the house hadn't had time to fall into rack and ruin. She had whizzed through the house with a feather duster and the vacuum cleaner that she had found in the large pantry next to the kitchen.

For a lone bachelor, Mitch's house was rather large. The living room alone was larger than most of her cabin. A huge fireplace across one entire wall was the center of attention. The cathedral ceiling lent an air of spatial elegance.

As she had thought, the furniture was mostly geared to a man's taste and Jenny wondered if it had always been so.

There were nine other rooms besides the formal living

room, all of them immense in size. Deep terra-cotta-colored carpeting wandered throughout the house, with the color scheme of every room blending with a complementary, harmonious mixture of rustic furniture and Native American. Definitely a man's home.

When she had arrived she'd decided to start with the kitchen so that she could have a meal cooking while she cleaned the rest of the house. Mitch's pantry afforded her a much larger choice than what she presently had in her own cupboards.

Now, reentering the kitchen, Jenny went to the pantry and put the cleaning supplies away. Pouring herself a glass of iced tea, she plopped down into a chair. A glance at her watch told her she still had twenty minutes.

She nervously tapped her fingers on the tabletop. After a few minutes she got up to check on the roast simmering in the oven. The meat was nestled in a bed of carrots, potatoes and onions. Its broth was rich and brown and gave off a mouthwatering aroma.

Closing the oven door, she thought she heard the sound of a vehicle in the driveway. Looking at her watch again, she realized it could only be Mitch. Her stomach seemed to squeeze within her. Her hands started to shake. Taking a deep breath steadied her enough to allow her to go to the front door and open it.

Mitch descended from the Jeep, walked to the back and pulled out a small suitcase. Moving around to the passenger side, he helped his mother from the car. After she alighted, she stood staring transfixed at the landscape in front of her eyes.

"It's so different."

Jenny could barely catch the whispered words.

Mitch motioned with his hands.

"Come inside out of the cold," he told her, his voice more chilling than the air surrounding them. "I want you to meet someone."

Without touching her, he led her over to where Jenny waited patiently. The two women stared at one another, each trying to assess the other.

Jenny for her part was surprised. From the things she had heard, she had expected his mother to be stylishly dressed and with faultless makeup. What she saw was a small, middle-aged woman wearing a conservative skirt and jacket and low-heeled pumps. Although she held her age well, she had done nothing to hold back Father Time, and her eyes had delicate laugh lines at the corners. The eyes arrested her attention more than anything else. A perpetual sadness seemed to lurk in their emerald-green depths.

From a picture Mitch had sitting on his mantel, she knew that Mitch was the spitting image of his father. One look, though, and it was apparent from where he'd inherited his eyes.

"This is Jenny Gordon, our neighbor. Jenny, Delores Anderson."

Neither woman missed the conspicuous neglect of title where his mother was concerned.

"How do you do?" Jenny extended her hand.

"Hello. Mitch has told me about you. It was kind of you to offer to look after things while his housekeeper had to be away."

"I was glad to do it." She frowned at Mitch. He was doing nothing to make his mother feel at home.

Mitch's eyes darkened with suppressed emotion. He strode up the veranda stairs and through the front door. Delores followed him, still looking around her.

"I can't believe how much things have changed."

Jenny followed Delores into the house, walked past her and headed for the kitchen. She had never felt so uncomfortable in her life.

Mitch emerged from a bedroom down the hallway where

he had taken his mother's suitcase. His face seemed carved in stone.

"I put your things in your bedroom. I had the house re-decorated years ago so feel free to explore in case you don't remember where things are."

Although nothing was said about her years of absence, the implication was clear. Jenny could see the hurt that flashed momentarily through Delores's eyes. Nodding, she passed Mitch, her shoulders slumped in dejection, and went to the end of the hallway.

Jenny and Mitch stood uncomfortably, waiting in silence. Mitch finally turned to her.

"Thanks for cleaning the house. Everything looks great. Something smells good, too."

The tension in the air was stifling. Jenny wanted to protest his treatment of his mother, but she knew she hadn't the right. This was something they were going to have to work out together.

Before she could think of anything to say, she heard muffled crying coming from Delores's bedroom. Jenny watched the color drain from Mitch's face. He quickly schooled his features into a rigid mask of self-control before turning and walking out the front door. She heard the Jeep start up before it peeled out of the driveway.

Now where on earth was Mitch going? She couldn't believe that he had just left her here alone with his mother. Standing helplessly in the middle of the room, Jenny was uncertain what to do. She should be leaving. Renee and David would be home soon and she needed to be there. Hesitating, she finally made a decision and strode purposefully down the hall. There was something pitiful and touching about the way Delores was trying to control her sobbing.

Pausing a moment at the door, it occurred to Jenny that perhaps Delores wouldn't appreciate being intruded upon. Her sad weeping came plaintively, though muffled, through the partially closed door.

Taking a deep breath, Jenny pushed the door open hesitantly and stopped on the threshold. The sight of Delores Anderson kneeling beside her bed with her head buried in the covers brought a lump to Jenny's throat. Gone was the poised, elegant woman of yesteryear. These were not pretend tears. They were the soul-cleansing tears of a woman leaving the past behind.

Jenny went to her and placed a hand on her shoulder. She tried to understand what Delores was saying through her moaning.

"I gave it all up. I was so selfish."

Jenny stood quietly, offering silent sympathy.

Delores lifted her head from the covers and Jenny saw a pain-ravaged face that seemed older than before. Mascara was smeared in all directions, giving her a grotesquely fiendish appearance.

Jenny's heart went out to her. She hated to see anything in pain. Although this woman had caused immense sorrow herself, her anguish was genuine and Jenny had no desire to see her suffer more.

"You came to ask forgiveness, didn't you?" she asked softly.

Delores nodded her head slowly, her tears starting to subside.

"Do you think he'll ever forgive me? Do you think he can?"

"I don't know." Gently, Jenny helped Delores to her feet and led her to the bathroom. She seated her on an antique chair in the corner. Pulling a washcloth from the stack on the counter, she turned on the faucet and soaked it with cold water. Handing it to Delores, she leaned against the edge of the counter.

"Why did you wait all these years?" Jenny didn't recognize the hoarse voice as her own.

Delores smiled wryly, looking down at the floor.

"I wanted to come back. I started to several times, but

I just couldn't bring myself to do it. I've been so selfish. All my life I never cared about anyone but myself. I never wanted Mitch." She looked up at Jenny. If she was looking for a horrified reaction, she received it.

Jenny was astounded. "How could you not want your own baby?"

Delores stared at the washcloth in her hand, twisting it slowly around.

"I was selfish. I didn't know any other way. I was an only child and my parents spoiled me horribly. Anything I wanted was given to me. Mitch was just someone who got in my way." She looked up at Jenny, a half smile playing around her lips. "Whatever you do, don't spoil your kids."

"But you came back. Why now? Why after all these years?"

Getting up, Delores crossed to Jenny. She placed an urgent hand on Jenny's arm.

"I need to talk to someone. If I tell you something, will you promise not to tell anyone?" She squeezed Jenny's hand lightly. "Not anyone."

This was something Jenny hadn't counted on. She had never intended to get involved. Even now, the rational part of her brain was telling her not to get mixed up in something that didn't concern her.

But didn't it? She loved Mitch. If there was any way to bring about reconciliation between Mitch and his mother, shouldn't she try? She wanted to help him. For that matter, she wanted to help Delores Anderson, as well. Whatever she had been like in the beginning, Jenny could see that Delores was not the woman she had once been.

Looking intently into Delores's eyes she told her, "I won't tell anyone if you don't want me to."

Delores's shoulders sagged with relief. She leaned heavily against the sink for support and Jenny became alarmed.

"Are you all right?"

A wry smile crooked Delores's lips, making her look so much like her son, it caused Jenny a pang.

"No," she told her softly. "I'm not all right. I'm dying."

Jenny felt a cold chill rush through her. "Dying?"

Delores nodded. "I have cancer. I waited too long for treatment, and now the doctors tell me I only have six weeks to live. Maybe a little more, maybe a little less."

Jenny stood uncertainly, hands clenching and unclenching at her sides as she tried to think of how to respond. "Are you going to tell Mitch?"

"I haven't decided yet." Delores straightened away from the counter, laying the washcloth out to dry. "It depends on how things go between us."

Jenny was angry now. "But you have to tell him. Do you know what this could do to him?"

"Jenny?" Mitch's anxious voice came from the living room, interrupting their talk.

Delores clenched Jenny's hand with her own. "Remember. You promised not to tell."

Jenny studied her for a long moment before she reluctantly nodded her head. She left Delores in the bathroom and went to find Mitch. He was just coming from the kitchen.

"There you are," he said in relief.

Jenny glared at him. "What was the big idea leaving me here like that? You ought to be ashamed of yourself."

Lips pressed into a tight line, Mitch shook his head. "I'm sorry. I didn't know what to do." His voice lowered to a husky whisper. "I can handle anything but tears."

Wetting her lips, Jenny reached for her coat without looking at him. He only *thought* he could handle anything. He had no idea what agony he was about to experience. She so wanted to warn him, but she had given her word.

"I have to go now, Mitch. The twins will be home soon."

He watched her, his hands curled into fists at his sides. "Your supper is in the oven. It should be ready anytime you want to eat it," she told him, buttoning her coat. She had to get out of here before she said something she shouldn't.

Mitch swallowed convulsively. "You could stay for supper. I could go get the twins."

Jenny shook her head, advancing to the door. "No. You and your mother have things you need to talk about." Twisting the doorknob, she told him, "There's a salad in the refrigerator and a coconut cake on the counter." She caught his eye, her heart twisting at the pain she saw there. "Give her a chance, Mitch," she whispered, quickly closing the door behind her.

For the next several days Jenny fell into a kind of routine. After she got the twins off to school, she went to Mitch's to make sure everything was staying clean and to fix the evening meal. Of Mitch there was no sign. Jenny assumed he left early and returned late. She had no idea where he disappeared to each day.

After the third day, Delores came into the kitchen and climbed onto one of the stools pulled up to the stove island. She pulled a bowl of fruit toward her, taking out an apple.

"You're in love with my son, aren't you?" she asked, taking a bite of the fruit.

Jenny stared at her in alarm. If Delores could see that, could Mitch?

"Well, aren't you?" she insisted. "And don't tell me it's none of my business, either. I already got that from Mitch."

"You discussed this with Mitch?" she asked incredulously.

Delores nodded her head.

"What did he say?" Jenny asked curiously.

"I just told you. He told me to mind my own business."

"Well, I agree," Jenny told her, pulling the bowl of potatoes across the counter. Picking up the knife she started to peel one. Her fingers were shaking so badly she was afraid she would cut herself. Setting the knife back on the counter, she turned to Delores.

"How about you and Mitch? Have you told him yet?"

Delores smiled. "Changing the subject? That's okay. I already know the answer. You and Mitch are in love with each other but something is keeping you apart. I would be willing to bet that something has to do with me."

Jenny was surprised by her insight.

"Some," Jenny told her truthfully.

Delores pursed her lips. "Mitch is a rich man. He would be quite a catch."

Jenny turned on her, her eyes flashing fire. "I would love Mitch if he hadn't a dime to his name!"

Delores raised her eyebrows. "I figured as much, and thank you for answering my question."

Jenny blinked at her. How on earth had she managed to let the woman finagle *that* out of her?

"Look, can we talk about something else?" she asked in frustration, once again picking up her knife.

Getting up from the stool, Delores crossed to the counter. Pulling another knife from the drawer, she reached for a potato and started peeling it. Jenny stared at her in surprise.

Delores's lips quirked wryly. "Let me guess. Mitch told you I was helpless in the kitchen."

Jenny merely nodded.

"That might have been true once, but I've learned a lot over the years." She reached for another potato and deftly peeled it. "Mitch has no idea how I led my life after I left here. I suffered enough so that somewhere along the line, I decided that I didn't want to suffer *after* this life as well. It took me a while, but I eventually found the Lord."

Jenny's knife clattered to the floor. "Have you told Mitch this?"

Delores stooped and picked up Jenny's knife, handing it back to her. She smiled wryly.

"We haven't talked much. He kind of avoids me whenever possible."

"Mrs. Anderson, you have to tell him. You have to tell him everything." Pushing the potatoes aside, Jenny asked, "How long have you known the Lord?"

"Oh, about ten years now."

"Ten years! And you're just now coming to Mitch?"

"I figured he thought I was dead and that it would be better if I just left things that way."

Jenny shook her head sadly. "He was engaged a couple of years ago."

Delores stared at her intently. "And?"

"She left. She couldn't stand the isolation."

Leaning back against the counter, Delores let out a long breath. "Well, that explains a lot, doesn't it?"

Jenny looked away. Picking up the potatoes that were peeled, she headed for the sink.

"I'm going to suggest something to you, Jenny, and I hope you won't take it the wrong way."

Jenny turned, giving Delores her full attention. "Yes?"

"I'd like you not to bother coming here anymore. Just for a while, mind you."

Jenny was speechless with surprise.

"I can take over the cooking and cleaning while I'm here. And I intend to stay until Mitch can settle himself down and talk to me. I need some time alone with him. Some time to let him see how much I've changed. Can you understand?"

"I can understand," Jenny told her. "I think that's a great idea and, frankly, I'm kind of relieved."

Delores smiled at her. "I didn't say anything before because I wanted to get to know you. I could tell that something was brewing between you and Mitch."

Jenny flushed but didn't say anything. If something was brewing, it was definitely more on her part than his.

Working side by side, they finished supper together. As she was leaving, Jenny spontaneously hugged Delores.

"I hope things work out for you," she told her.

Pressing her lips together in a smile Delores replied, "They will. The good Lord will work it out somehow."

As Jenny was driving down the road she fervently prayed for a new understanding between mother and son. Only three more days until Christmas. Surely this was a time for amazing things to happen.

Chapter 12

Christmas Day arrived and with it one of the coldest days of the year. Although it was rare, predictions of snow made Jenny hesitate to make the trip to Hattie's. Low clouds hung over the horizon. Snow clouds. Normally they would bring rain, but the temperature precluded that. Either snow or ice would surely be falling within the next hour.

The sky got progressively darker over the next half hour. Jenny watched the sky anxiously for any signs of snow. She hated driving in bad weather.

She turned back to the room and smiled at the twins. David was busy playing with the computer game he had received for Christmas. Pings, pongs and squeaks echoed around the living room, mingled with the Christmas music drifting from Renee's CD player. She had wanted to give them each something special and with the check she had received this month, she had been able to.

The price Annie had put on the quilted wall hanging that she had named "Silent Night" had astounded Jenny.

That she had received it had boggled her mind even more. With the sale of that one item alone she had been able to buy David his computer game and several game cartridges.

The Christmas tree sat forlornly in the corner, already a has-been. Fudge, though, still thought it deserved some attention. Grabbing the popcorn string that had fallen too close to the bottom, he gave a mighty tug. The tree started to sway ever so gently and Jenny lunged at the same time Renee noticed and dived after Fudge.

Settling the tree back into its upright position, Jenny laughed as Renee scolded Fudge.

"Bad dog. That's a no-no."

Fudge's little tail curled between his legs as his ears pinned themselves close to his head. Jenny knew what the outcome would be before it even happened. Sure enough, Renee scooped the pup into her arms and was hugging him tightly.

"Be a good boy, okay?" she pleaded.

Jenny glanced at her new watch. The twins had gone in together to buy it for her, and she was proudly pleased to display it. She hadn't known that Renee had been tutoring during her study halls to make a little money. Along with the money David earned from Mitch, they had decided to purchase Jenny something extra special. Jenny couldn't have been more pleased if it had been diamond-encrusted with a pure gold band.

"It's about time we left."

Watching the gathering storm clouds she again felt a twinge of unease. By the time they were on the road, snow had started to fall in earnest. Huge, fluffy flakes bounced against her windshield. It was amazing how something so beautiful could be so dangerous.

When they arrived at Hattie's, the snow was already sticking to the ground. It had been fairly decent driving until she had hit the pavement, whereupon it had taken all her driving skill to stay on the icy road.

"It shouldn't last," Hattie told her, watching the sky. "Probably be over by the time you guys start for home."

Jenny certainly hoped she was right.

Celebrating with the Ameses turned out to be an enjoyable time and Jenny was glad now that they had come.

Placing dishes on the table for the evening meal, Hattie asked, "Have you heard anything from Mitch or Delores?"

"No. Have you?"

Hattie shook her head. "I invited them for Christmas, but they declined."

"Do you know what they planned for Christmas?" Jenny asked.

"No. I just hope…" She stopped and sighed. Jenny understood. From what she had seen, Mitch had done nothing toward making the holiday festive at his house.

Further discussion was delayed when April brought in the turkey resting in all its golden glory upon the traditional Christmas platter.

The remaining hours gave Jenny a glimpse of what it was like to be part of a loving family again. It was at times such as these that she felt the loss of her parents most intensely. It brought with it a longing for Mitch so deep it was like a physical pain. The presents, the games, the laughter, everything would have been perfect if Mitch could have been here to share in it with her.

As Jenny was preparing to leave later that evening, Hattie confronted her.

"Maybe you should stay, Jenny. The snow hasn't let up and it's unusually deep."

Jenny hesitated. She sure didn't want to endanger the twins' lives.

Renee tugged at her sleeve. "Fudge hasn't been fed. I don't want to leave him alone all night."

When Jenny checked outside, the snow was still swirling fast and furious. She hesitated, unsure whether to go or to stay. Jacob added his voice to Hattie's dissenting one. Still,

Jenny hesitated. For some reason she had an overwhelming desire to spend the final hours of Christmas in her own home. When she decided to go ahead and leave, Hattie made her promise to call as soon as they made it home.

After rounds of thank-yous and hugs, the three started on their way. Jenny hadn't gone very far before she realized she had made a big mistake.

Mitch reached for the telephone with an almost overwhelming premonition of trouble. His heart dropped to his stomach when he heard Hattie's urgent voice at the other end.

"Slow down, Hattie," he soothed. "I can't understand what you're saying."

He heard her take a deep breath. "Maybe it's nothing. I'm sure it is, but Jenny and the twins left here hours ago and she hasn't called to let me know they arrived safely."

Mitch was thankful that he was sitting, because all the muscles in his body seemed to suddenly be made of jelly.

"Did you try calling her?"

"Of course I did," she answered impatiently. Taking another breath she told him, "I'm sorry, Mitch. Yes, I've tried calling her several times but her phone goes straight to voice mail."

"The snow might be interfering with transmission from the cell tower. What on earth was she driving around in this stuff for, anyway?" Mitch stared out his living room window at the swirling mass of white. Of all the times to have record-breaking amounts of snow....

Hattie answered his question, although he hadn't really expected her to.

"They came to spend Christmas with us. I tried to get them to stay, but for some reason Jenny was adamant."

Mitch snorted, irritated and concerned at the same time. "That sounds like Jenny. She can be as stubborn as a little jenny donkey. They named her well."

His mother entered the room. "What is it, Mitch?"

Mitch glanced across the room at her. They had been having quite a talk. Something he would like to resume, as soon as he found out what had happened to Jenny.

He briefly related the situation while Hattie waited patiently at the other end.

"Okay, Hattie," he told her. "She has to be somewhere between your place and home. Maybe she pulled off the road when it got too bad. I'll go see if I can find her. It'll take me a little bit to get chains on my tires. I'll call you before I start out. If you hear from Jenny before then, give me a call on my cell."

He hung up the phone, staring off into space. It took a huge effort to get his feelings under control. It wouldn't help if he went out of here half-cocked. But the thought of Jenny out there in the snow with the twins spurred him into action.

As he put on his coat, his mother followed him into the entryway.

"Is there anything I can do?" she asked quietly.

He answered just as quietly before he opened the door that led into the garage. "Pray," he told her.

"I will."

Mitch stared at her a moment. She had just told him about making the Lord a part of her life and he had been so surprised he hadn't known what to say. Nothing short of an emergency would have induced him to interrupt their conversation.

"We'll finish our talk when I get home," he told her, hating to leave but knowing he must.

After years of practice, the tire chains went on with ease. The door to the garage opened and he stood staring in amazement at the sheet of white raining down from the sky. It was going to be difficult finding anything out in this. He took a deep breath, throwing up a prayer for Jenny and the twins. He checked to make certain Hattie hadn't tried to reach him, made sure all his emergency gear was in the Jeep, then, jumping in, he threw it into gear and took off in the direction of Jenny's ranch.

Mitch kept a firm rein on his thoughts as he slowly traversed the distance between Jenny's ranch and his. Fear, the likes of which he had never known before, threatened to overwhelm him if he allowed it access to his thoughts.

Jenny. His little Jenny. He realized that that was exactly how he considered her. If something happened to Jenny, he didn't know what he would do.

He had no words to express his chaotic thoughts so he settled for a heartfelt, *Father, please...*

The darkness made seeing difficult. Thankfully the snow began to lessen, improving his visibility. He had decided it would be easier to spot something if he drove in the middle of the road. Fortunately, traffic on this road was rare. As he crept along, his eyes strained to find anything out of the ordinary.

He drove with the windows down so he could see the sides of the road better, making the inside of the Jeep freezing cold. His sheepskin jacket and leather fur-lined gloves helped lessen the effect of the freezing temperatures and his heater was pushing air full blast, but the chill temperatures still hit him with ferocious intensity.

He was about four miles from the turnoff to Jenny's ranch and still had spotted nothing. The house had been empty when he finally arrived, causing his panic to surface a little more. They had to be somewhere between here and Hattie's.

Out of the corner of his eye he caught something off to his immediate left and he stopped the Jeep, got out and ran to investigate. What he saw made his heart catch, before resuming its rate at ten times its normal speed.

Jenny's little white Toyota had been hard to spot since it blended so well with the full, white landscape. It had slid off the road and managed to flip itself over onto the passenger side in a small culvert. Only a huge drift of snow had kept it from turning onto its roof.

Sliding down the bank, he realized the car was almost buried by snow. No movement came from within. No sound penetrated the still air around him.

"Jenny!" His voice sounded harsh to his own ears. "David! Renee!" He brushed frantically to remove the snow from the vehicle's doors.

"Mitch? Is that you?" David's voice seemed muffled and hesitant.

"Yes, it's me." *Thank You, Lord!* He deliberately made his voice louder. "Are you all right? Are Renee and Jenny with you?"

David's voice came back to him, almost frantic. "Renee's okay, but we can't get Jenny to wake up! Her head's bleeding."

Pushing down the panic that was threatening to take over, Mitch tugged open the driver's door. He could see Jenny hanging in her seat belt at an awkward angle. Looking past her he found David pushed against the passenger door. Renee was crying softly, curled into the back corner of the vehicle.

"Are you okay?" he asked them as his hands gently worked their way across Jenny's body. As far as he could tell, the wound on her head was her only injury. But then, he was no expert.

"Just a little bruised," David answered. "But what about Jenny?"

"I don't know. I'm afraid to move her, but if I don't, she will freeze."

Pulling out his phone, he tried to get a signal but there was none. It was possible that a 9-1-1 call would ping off a satellite and get through, but how long would it take an emergency vehicle to get through to this isolated spot? He hesitated, momentarily unsure of what to do. If he moved her, he could possibly cause her more injury, perhaps irreparable damage. Renee's chattering teeth made his decision.

"David. Can you climb over the seat and come out the back door? I'll hold it open for you. Can you and Renee both do that?"

David slowly unwound his body, sucking in a painful breath. Gritting his teeth, he climbed slowly, clumsily, onto the backseat. Renee tried to help him.

Mitch slowly closed the driver's door. Grasping the back door, he jerked it open and held it with his shoulder. Reaching in with both hands, he helped Renee climb over David and out of the car. David was slower to follow. Mitch could see he was in pain. He helped him as much as he could, but his position was somewhat precarious.

When David was standing beside Renee, Mitch allowed the door to close. Glancing quickly at David, and noting the extreme pallor of his face, he determined that he would get little help from that quarter.

"Renee, I'm going to need your help."

David protested, but Mitch wasn't about to argue. David's color and raspy breathing was beginning to alarm him.

"I want you to go sit in the Jeep."

"I need to help Jenny!" His voice was a thread of a whisper.

"Do it, David!"

Without waiting to see if he had been obeyed, Mitch turned back to the car.

"Okay, Renee. I need you to hold the door open. Do you think you can do that?"

She nodded, reaching to hold the handle, which Mitch relinquished to her. Climbing onto the side of the car, Mitch straddled the door. Bending down and leaning his upper torso way into the car, he slowly undid Jenny's seat belt. He felt her body sag against his arm, almost catching him off-balance. Taking a firmer grip, he pulled her from the car as gently as possible. He was thankful that she was unconscious. There was no telling what pain he might have caused her otherwise.

Lifting her into his arms, he swiftly plowed through the thickening snow and crossed the road, Renee trotting beside him.

Pulling open the back door of the Jeep, he glanced quickly at David, whose head was resting against the rolled-up passenger window in the front seat. The raspy sound of his breathing concerned Mitch.

"Sit in the back, Renee. I'll lay Jenny across your lap. Hang on to her. I'll have to go quickly, but I'll try not to jar her too much."

Renee clambered onto the backseat. "Will she be okay?"

"I don't know. We'll just pray real hard. Okay?"

Renee gave him a tentative smile and nodded her head. As Mitch set Jenny into her care, she looked at her brother for confirmation, but he didn't answer.

Once in the driver's seat, Mitch leaned across the seat and lifted the lid of David's eye. The pupil was dilated and unresponsive. Shock and pain had rendered him semiconscious. There had to be more wrong with David than mere bruises.

Mitch started the Jeep and shifted into gear in one quick movement. Thank God he had remembered his snow chains. He would need to head for the nearest hospital, and that meant traveling on the freeway. He only hoped that the snowplows had already cleared the road.

It seemed to Mitch that they were crawling along, but he knew that wasn't so. The freeway had been cleared of snow and he had been able to travel quickly, but it wasn't quickly enough for him. The only thing that kept him from doing something foolish and putting his foot down hard on the accelerator was the three precious lives in his care.

Pulling into the hospital emergency entrance, he realized that almost two hours had passed since he had left his ranch. He had no idea how long Jenny and the twins had been trapped in the car with no heat.

Shoving open his door, he swiftly crossed the parking area and disappeared inside the building. Moments later he emerged with a hospital crew and two gurneys.

What followed was the worst nightmare Mitch had ever experienced; short of the time his mother had abandoned him. The weeks he had spent sitting at the window, watching for her return, had seemed an eternity. Now the time seemed to drag by just as slowly as he waited for Jenny, Renee and David to be examined. The antiseptic smell that permeated all hospitals brought back painful memories of the past. His father had died of complications resulting from cancer surgery while he had been waiting in just such a room. Mitch hated hospitals.

Before long Renee joined him in the waiting room. He studied her carefully. "Are you all right?"

"Just some bruises," she told him.

Sitting next to him, she reached her hand across and curled her fingers around his. Turning his head, he tried to smile reassuringly, giving her fingers a gentle squeeze. They both waited in silence; it was comforting for each of them just to be near one another.

After what seemed an eternity, a white-coated doctor appeared. Mitch breathed a sigh of relief as he recognized his friend from church. The man strode across the room, pulling up in front of them. Mitch got to his feet.

"How is he, James?"

"David has several fractured ribs. The position he was in caused them to puncture his right lung. Fortunately, it's not too serious. He should be fine. Barring complications, and depending on how long it takes to reinflate the lung, he should be able to go home in four or five days."

Mitch nodded. "And Jenny?"

The doctor shook his head. "I don't know. My colleague

is with her right now. He'll let you know when he finishes examining her."

"Thanks, James. When can we see David?"

"He's sedated right now for the pain. You can see him later, when he wakes up."

Mitch swallowed hard as James exited the room. He hadn't realized how much he had grown to love the young teen. He glanced at Renee and realized that he loved the whole Gordon family. He wanted to protect and care for them all, and not just now. He gritted his teeth at his helplessness in controlling the situation, and turned to stare hollowly at the door.

It was some time later before the doctor appeared. Renee had curled up on the sofa and was fast asleep. The best medicine for shock, James had assured Mitch. Mitch gently draped his jacket across her. Leaving her there, he met the other doctor in the doorway.

"Well?"

"You're James's friend, the one who found them?"

Mitch nodded.

"My name is Adams. Dr. Benjamin Adams."

He held out his hand and Mitch clasped it briefly. He seemed to be studying Mitch before he gave a brief smile. "Jenny has a severe concussion. My main concern is not for that, but the huge loss of blood from her head wound. The fact that the temperatures were so cold probably kept her from bleeding to death."

Thank the Lord for freezing temperatures, Mitch thought.

"Will she be okay?"

"Her vitals are good, though a bit sluggish. We'll watch her carefully tonight and be able to tell you more in the morning."

"Can I see her?"

Dr. Adams hesitated.

"I know I'm not her husband, but I'd really like to see her. Just for a few minutes."

The doctor heaved a sigh before reluctantly nodding his permission.

"But only for five minutes. I must warn you, she hasn't regained consciousness."

Mitch watched him walk away before turning to Renee. He gently shook her shoulder. Slowly she opened sleep-drugged eyes.

"We can see Jenny now."

Staring down at Jenny's swathed form, Mitch felt a tightening in his chest. She looked so tiny. So vulnerable. He lifted her small hand from the covers and held it between his own two larger ones.

Renee stood on the other side of the bed and suddenly burst into tears. Mitch quickly replaced Jenny's hand on the bed and swiftly went to Renee's side, pulling her gently into his arms.

"Shh." He rocked her back and forth. "We can't disturb her, you know."

Renee continued to sob against his shirt. "Please don't let her die. Please don't let her die."

Mitch was unsure whether she was talking to him or asking for Divine intervention. Nevertheless he pulled her from the room and led her back to the waiting room. Seating her in a chair, he squatted in front of her.

"She's not going to die, Renee. God won't let that happen."

She buried her face in her hands, rocking herself back and forth on the chair. "He let my parents die."

The bitter accusation hung in the air between them. He wasn't sure what to say to such a statement. How could he explain that bad things happen, but that didn't make it God's fault, especially when it suddenly occurred to him that he had been doing the same thing for many years?

For the first time he realized that ever since his mother had left him, he had blamed God for it. Knowing in his mind it wasn't true didn't stop the feeling inside that God could have somehow prevented it. He could certainly empathize with Renee's feelings.

Reaching out, he lifted her hands away from her face, curling his strong fingers around them and giving them a slight shake.

"I don't know if I can explain this or not. Maybe I'm not the best one to try. Do you remember in Brother Taylor's sermon Sunday that he talked about how Paul had written the Romans that all things work together for the good of those who love the Lord?"

"I remember."

"Paul didn't say *most* things, and he didn't say *some* things. He said *all* things."

Renee looked unconvinced. "How can Jenny's being hurt be good?"

Mitch smiled. "It doesn't say all things are good, Renee, only that it will work out for good. The bad things that happen refine us, prepare us for the good God has in store for us."

The thought uppermost in Mitch's mind right now was that if he had married Amanda, by now they would both be miserable and he would have been stuck when Jenny walked into his life. The thought of life without Jenny didn't bear thinking about.

"How can my parents' death work for good?" she asked hopelessly.

"I don't know how it will work out for your good, but for me, it brought you into my life. In the book of Job it tells us that a man's days are numbered. We all have an appointment with death, Renee, and even though your parents' appointment was earlier than we would have wished, God knew that I would be there to take up the slack. I'm here for you, Renee." He didn't know what else to say. "We just have to have faith," he told her, knowing that it had been sadly lacking in his life. Thankfully, God hadn't given up on him.

Renee pulled her hands from Mitch's clasp. She leaned back in the chair and closed her eyes. She looked so tired, so utterly forlorn.

"I'll be okay if you want to go see Jenny."

He realized he needed to give her time to think about what he had just said, so he left her alone and went back to Jenny's room. He stayed only a moment.

She laid still and quiet, her face pale against the white hospital sheets. He felt so completely helpless. He was a man of action, and it was frustrating to know that there was nothing more he could do, other than pray. It occurred to him that he hadn't been doing much of that lately, either. Maybe he hadn't really believed that God would truly listen. If he was honest with himself, he knew that he hadn't been the kind of true Christian that he should have been. He had only been going through the motions.

Bowing his head, he prayed, "Father, forgive me for pushing You away all these years. Help me to be the godly man You meant for me to be. And please, let Jenny get better and give me another chance to apologize to her and tell her just how much I love her."

Bending, he kissed Jenny softly on the lips. He leaned his forehead gently against her bandaged one a moment before he turned and walked out of the room.

He found David in a room much like Jenny's. Breathing equipment was connected to him, tubes snaking in several directions.

When Mitch padded softly across to the bed, David's eyes slowly opened. The boy smiled a lopsided smile.

"How's Jen?" His dry, cracked voice pleaded for reassurance.

"So far, so good. It's a good thing she has such a hard head, huh?" Mitch's attempt to lighten a serious situation had the desired effect. A slight grin touched David's mouth and he tried to nod his head, flinching at the discomfort.

"How are you doing, buddy?" Mitch asked, noting that a little color had returned to his face.

"I'm okay. Just a little sleepy."

Reaching out, Mitch pushed back the damp tendrils of hair curled across David's forehead.

"Go to sleep, then. Everything will be all right."

"What about Renee?" David croaked.

"Renee's fine. Just a little banged up. She wants to see you, but I think I'll have her wait till morning. Get some rest, okay?"

Mitch watched his eyes close slowly before returning to the waiting room. He found Renee much as he had left her.

She accepted Mitch's explanation that David was resting and was doing fine, and that she could see him first thing in the morning.

They found a hotel in downtown Prescott and registered for the night. Mitch walked Renee to her door, which was next to his own. He pulled her into a reassuring embrace, kissing her on the forehead and reminding her again that he was there for her.

She gave him a tired smile.

"Lock your door," he admonished softly, pushing her gently into the room. "And try to get some rest."

After waiting until she closed and locked the door behind her, Mitch went to his own room and called Hattie. He made arrangements for the next morning before hanging up and walking to his bed. Without undressing, he lay down on the covers and stared up at the ceiling.

Chapter 13

When Jenny was finally released from the hospital, she came home with less energy than she could ever remember having. She spent the largest part of her days reclining on the sofa and contemplating the future.

Since the accident, she'd been struggling with fears she hadn't considered before. What if she had died? What would have happened to the twins? What if David had died? Or Renee? So far away from any people, it could have happened. If Mitch hadn't come along when he had, she would probably be dead now, and possibly David and Renee, as well. Every time she thought about it, her blood went cold.

For the first time in a long while her faith had been shaken. Not since before her acceptance of the Lord into her life had her faith wavered in such a way. She felt guilty. What kind of Christian was she that at the first sign of trouble she doubted her Lord? She knew in her heart that God had not abandoned her, but her head was getting in her way.

January blew in as cold as December. The lack of heat

in the cabin was beginning to aggravate her. They could freeze. Her incoherent thoughts raged on, making her more and more dissatisfied with her life. Summer would soon come and with it the almost unbearable heat. Things that hadn't bothered her before now loomed like a giant monster just waiting to devour her shaking faith.

Jenny seriously considered selling the ranch and moving somewhere else. It never occurred to her that a large part of her dissatisfaction had to do with the fact that she hadn't seen Mitch since the day before she'd left the hospital. Hattie had been the one to bring her home. Why was he staying away? It only proved to her that he had no real feelings for her. Were it the other way around, nothing in the world would have kept her from him.

Jenny had no way of knowing that Mitch was having an emergency of his own. He was standing even now in the same waiting room where he had waited for news of Jenny and David.

His mother had collapsed only days after Jenny's return. It had come as a shock to Mitch to find out that she was dying of inoperable lung cancer. He had wondered at her lack of appetite and worried at her loss of weight, but had attributed it to being isolated at his ranch again. He had assumed that she was dying to leave, and instead she had been literally dying. How ironic that when he had finally come to believe in her ability to change, when he was finally able to forgive and have her back as his mother, she might be leaving him for good. Thank God they had resolved their differences. What saddened Mitch the most was the thought of all those wasted years.

Sitting, he buried his face in his hands. Heaving a great sigh of regret he pleaded with God to let him have more time with his mother. He wanted so much. He wanted her to be able to experience her own grandchildren. She had spoken of that often in the days before her collapse.

But that was not to be. That day Delores Anderson died quietly in her sleep without ever having awakened from the coma she had slipped into. Hattie was with Mitch at the hospital when it happened. She wrapped her arms around Mitch's neck. He resisted but a moment, before pulling her close and burying his face in her neck. The sobs that shook his body made him realize that he truly had forgiven his mother for all the pain of the past.

Jenny heard a car coming up the track and her heart did a hopeful little hop.

"I wonder who that could be."

She glanced from Renee to David in time to catch the look that passed between them.

"What's going on?"

They shrugged their shoulders, hastily getting up from their seats.

"I have some homework to do," Renee told her, heading for their bedroom.

"Me, too," David agreed.

Since she normally had to coerce David to do his homework any other time, she was skeptical. Something was definitely wrong and she headed for the door with a near premonition of impending disaster.

Hattie was just emerging from her car, the lack of a smile causing Jenny a twinge of alarm. Her vivacious personality was more subdued than Jenny had ever seen it. Something terrible must have happened, and the twins seemed to know about it. Butterflies flittered in her stomach as she studied Hattie's set face.

Jenny invited her in, offering her a seat. It was impossible to miss Hattie's nervousness as she twisted a handkerchief through her fingers and refused to meet Jenny's eyes.

"What's wrong?" Jenny asked, getting right to the point.

Hattie leaned forward in her seat. "I have something I need to tell you about Mitch."

Jenny felt her heart constrict, her eyes widening in alarm. If anything happened to Mitch…

Hattie hesitated and Jenny had to stifle the urge to reach out and shake her.

"What is it?"

"Mitch's mother died last week."

Jenny felt the blood drain from her already pale face.

"Are you all right?" Hattie asked anxiously, reaching across and squeezing Jenny's hand.

Was she all right? Right now she felt like a wooden statue, with just about as much life in her. Renee and David came and sat to each side of her, their desire to comfort her touching her deeply.

"Why didn't anyone tell me?" she whispered.

"I'm afraid that's my fault," Hattie said softly. "I was afraid it would cause problems. Mitch agreed with me."

Jenny understood their concern. After the accident, she had been a shell of her normal self. No wonder they questioned whether she could handle such news. "When is the funeral?"

"Tomorrow. If you'd like to go, I'll come pick you up."

Jenny sat in stupefied silence, nodding her head. So much seemed to have happened in such a short time. Her perfect little world seemed to be falling apart at the seams.

A cold January wind tore through the solemn crowd of people who had come for Mitch's mother's funeral. The funeral had been a somber affair, short but eloquent. His mother had been remitted into the hands of the God she loved.

Amanda stood beside Mitch, her false show of concern grating on his already raw nerves. She had twined her arm through his and although he wanted to firmly push her away, he didn't want to cause a scene. Her attitude of late had made it clear that she would like to take up where they had left off. He was going to have to make it clear to her that there was no way that was going to happen.

He glanced up and caught the look on Jenny's face and his heart dropped. Surely she didn't think there was anything between Amanda and him. Although he had to admit that it was his own fault for bringing Amanda into the equation in the first place. He was going to have to talk to Jenny and get things out in the open once and for all. He was utterly tired of the dance they had been doing lately. Hopefully he would get a chance to talk to her before he had to leave on his afternoon flight.

When the service ended, he accepted the condolences of his friends, using the excuse to remove himself from Amanda's cloying presence. He turned to search for Jenny, but she had already disappeared. Gritting his teeth in frustration, he wove his way through the crowd and reluctantly headed for home.

Although his mother hadn't been with him long, the place was going to be lonely without her. He had grown used to coming home and finding her waiting with a meal, listening to his itinerary of the day's events.

In her final days they had discussed many things. He was going to trust his mother's judgment that Jenny was in love with him. Perhaps he was being a gullible fool, but he had decided that she was someone worth fighting for.

Before he could make that happen, though, he would have to go to San Francisco to settle his mother's affairs. It wasn't something he was looking forward to, but it was something that needed to be done and he was the only one able to do it.

Amanda followed him to his Jeep and although he wanted to find Jenny before his plane left, he knew he had to make this final break with Amanda. He had long been regretting his decision to invite her to his barbecue. It was time to make it perfectly clear to his former fiancée that he was head over heels in love with another woman.

* * *

A few days after Delores Anderson's funeral Annie had come to Jenny with a proposition. If Jenny would be willing to help Annie with her upcoming wedding, she would pay her enough to cover the costs of the time it lessened for making her crafts to sell.

At first Jenny was skeptical about being able to pull off such an affair, but with Hattie and Annie helping, she had finally agreed. It also gave her something to do to keep her mind off the fact that she had learned that Mitch had left town with Amanda.

When she had seen them together at the funeral, she had wondered if they were renewing their relationship. Now she had no doubt. Remembering Mitch's kisses, she felt used all over again, but this time the pain was ten times worse. The question was, how long did it take to mend a broken heart?

Despite her inner turmoil, the days flew by on wings. Jenny was kept so busy, she had little time to think and worry. Only three days remained till the wedding, and if Annie had her way, it was going to be the wedding of the century.

Jenny lifted the cream satin from her lap and gently shook it out. She held it up and critically studied every detail. Perfect. She couldn't be more pleased if it were her own dress. Annie would be thrilled. Thankfully she had finished it in time as Annie was on her way to pick it up today.

It wasn't long until she heard a vehicle rumbling up to her cabin. One thing she had always appreciated about their distance from the road was that it was impossible for company to take her unawares. Except, perhaps, if you were busy with coyotes and scorpions. She smiled at the memory, her smile fading as she thought of all that had transpired since that time. Love had been a painful experience for her.

She met Annie at the door, giving her a hug and inviting her in. Jenny lifted the dress carefully from the sofa, where she had it spread out for Annie to view it, and waited nervously for her to say something.

Annie inspected the dress, smiling. "It's perfect," she said breathlessly. "Oh, Jenny, it's absolutely gorgeous!"

Relieved, Jenny returned her smile. "Thank you. I thought so. You're going to make a beautiful bride."

Annie blushed, her dimples showing as her smile grew. The smile left her face and her look turned serious. "You've been a great friend, Jenny. I want you to know how much I've appreciated our friendship."

"As have I," Jenny agreed. She didn't know what she would have done without Hattie and Annie. God had blessed her in so many ways, not least of which was with remarkable friends.

Annie refused an offer to stay and visit. "There's a winter storm advisory. I need to get back to town before it hits and I still have a ton of things to do tonight."

Jenny followed her out onto the porch. She could see the dark, heavy clouds moving in from the northeast. The days had warmed to record temperatures, but the temperatures had been dropping steadily for the past hour. That would mean freezing temperatures and, if not snow, then definitely icy rain in the next few hours.

She watched Annie disappear down the road and decided to follow. Grabbing her purse from the coffee table and extracting her keys, she decided to pick up the twins early at Mitch's instead of waiting for him to bring them home.

It had been two weeks since Mitch had left town with Amanda and she had only heard about his return yesterday when the twins told her Mitch would be stopping by to pick them up in the morning. After sewing long hours into the night, she had been asleep when David and Renee had quietly slipped out of the house. Her stomach churned at the thought of facing him again, but she stiffened her spine, castigating herself for her timidity.

Reluctantly she started the engine. The desire to see Mitch warred with an equal desire to flee from him any time he was near. Every time she thought about her response to his kisses, she cringed inside. She had made it only too clear that all he had to do was snap his fingers and she was his for the taking. And to what purpose? He wanted her ranch. That was the only thing that made any sense, especially now that Amanda was back in his life. Yet when she had asked Annie to offer it to him after her stay in the hospital, he had refused point-blank, leaving her more confused than ever.

Pulling up in front of the ranch house, Jenny stopped the car and turned off the engine. She had learned from experience not to let it keep running, because there was no telling where the twins might be.

She waited several moments and had just decided to go searching when Mitch came out of the stables, David and Renee following behind. Fudge trotted close on Renee's heels. Mitch was leading a small colt that Jenny recognized as the one that had been born this past summer.

Seeing her car, all three stopped in their tracks. The colt tried to use the opportunity to show her independence, but Mitch stroked her soothingly, bringing her into submission. It was a poignant reminder of that first night when he had soothed her fears, as well.

Their eyes met across the distance and Jenny's heart turned over at the emotion she saw registered on his face. How could he look at her that way if he had feelings for Amanda? Or was it just wishful thinking on her part that made it seem as though something was there that really wasn't?

The moment disintegrated when the twins raced to the car, both talking at once.

"Hold on!" Jenny pleaded. "I can't understand a word you're saying."

Renee reached down to lift Fudge into her arms.

"I'll tell her," David said. Turning back to Jenny, his eyes alight, he said, "Mitch said I could spend the night if it's okay with you."

Jenny felt her heart sink. Rarely did she try to intervene in the relationship between Mitch and her brother, but David had to start getting used to being without the big man, especially if he married Amanda. She had made it quite clear that she wasn't particularly fond of children.

"Not tonight, David."

The light left his eyes and a mutinous expression tightened his features.

"Why not?"

Before she could answer, Mitch joined the group. He nodded his head at her. "Jenny."

Looking at David he asked him, "What's the matter?"

"Jenny says no." His voice was laced with venom and Jenny inwardly quailed at the coming confrontation.

Mitch studied Jenny momentarily before putting his hand on David's shoulder. Never taking his eyes from Jenny's face, he told David, "Well, if Jenny says no, then no it is."

David's mouth dropped open, but he was no more surprised than Jenny. She could see the words cramming for release from her brother. It was obvious he felt the subject far from closed.

"I'm sure she has her reasons," Mitch told him. He was looking at her again in that way that made her glad she was sitting. It was definitely time to leave.

"As a matter of fact, I do. I have a date tonight, and I don't want Renee to be alone."

Three pairs of surprised eyes fastened on her face. Mitch's lips pressed into a grim line. "Jenny, we need to talk."

Not if her life depended on it. "I'm sorry, Mitch. Maybe another time. I don't want to be late."

The silence went on until Jenny squirmed uncomfortably. Mitch's look told her the conversation was far from ended. Turning to David, Mitch put an arm around his shoulders. "Maybe another time, partner."

David nodded, crawling into the backseat. When Jenny turned to him, he looked away, his very posture announcing his displeasure. She sighed before glancing once again at Mitch.

"Thanks for having them."

He gave a curt nod, moving away from the car. "I guess I'll see you at Annie's wedding."

She reached forward and started the engine, in a hurry now just to get away.

Renee climbed into the front seat, cuddling Fudge close. She flicked a glance at David, Jenny and Mitch but remained silent.

The return trip to the cabin was a cold, silent one. David slammed into the house and Jenny blew out a frustrated breath. Renee gave her a sympathetic look, following her brother inside.

David was still not speaking to her when Jenny left the house. By now, she was irritated at the whole mess. Now was not the time to tell the twins that her *date* was with Annie to finish working on the centerpieces for the reception tables. She felt guilty at misleading Mitch, but she hadn't truly lied.

Annie walked down the aisle on the arm of her father, a rather formidable-looking gentleman. She was absolutely stunning. Her Gibson-style wedding dress was set off to perfection by a quaint Gibson hairstyle. Little blond ringlets curled becomingly around her cheeks. She looked at least ten years younger than her thirty-five years.

It had always amazed Jenny that someone as lovely as Annie would wait so long to marry. Seeing the love shine from her eyes, and the answering love from Jeremy's, Jenny could at last understand why. Annie had waited for God to send the right man.

The lovely ceremony brought tears to Jenny's eyes, which were drawn like a magnet toward Mitch. Her heart started thumping madly when she realized he was watching her. Amanda was nowhere to be seen. What exactly did that mean?

Jenny's attention shifted when she and Renee were grouped together with all the other eligible young ladies present. Giggling among themselves, Jenny couldn't help but respond to their lively chatter, her spirits lifting considerably.

"Okay, everyone. Get ready," Annie ordered as she turned her back. Glancing briefly over her left shoulder, she flung her bouquet unerringly in Jenny's direction.

Instinctively, Jenny reached out and caught the bouquet. Her face flushed with mortification as the crowd around her cheered.

"You caught it, Jenny!" Renee told her excitedly. "That means you'll be next."

Jenny lifted embarrassed eyes, only to encounter Mitch's intense green ones. Expecting to see mockery, she was surprised at the tenderness she saw there. Everything receded into the background as they continued to stare at each other. The laughing girls surging around her to congratulate her ended their silent exchange.

The winter storm that had been predicted days earlier had finally turned into a reality. Sleet had already begun to fall as they exited the church building after the reception. High winds seemed to push the cold right through to her very bones. Jenny shivered, wrapping her coat tightly around her.

Still feeling guilty over not allowing David to spend the night with Mitch, Jenny had relented and allowed him instead to spend tonight with Mark. When he walked away, it was clear that he was still not happy with her. She turned to her sister.

"The weatherman says a cold front is moving through. It's supposed to rain all night," she told her. "We'd better hurry and get home. The roads are going to be a mess."

From what the meteorologist had said, this was going to be no ordinary storm system. The weather had warmed to record temperatures and now an icy cold front was moving in from behind, bringing high winds and freezing rain.

It was as good an excuse as any to flee before Mitch could track her down and have that talk he had suggested. She didn't know what he wanted to say, but her heart was too sore right now to stay around to find out. She needed time to strengthen her defenses before she would have the courage to face him again.

The rain was coming down in buckets by the time they reached the house. Renee rushed inside while Jenny took a moment to move her potted plants closer up the porch against the walls of the cabin. Already the low-lying area behind the house looked like a small lake.

Jenny had to push hard against the howling wind to get the door to close. She was shaking the water from her coat when Renee suddenly leaped from the couch.

"Where's Fudge?"

Jenny looked at her. "Isn't he here?"

"I wasn't paying attention. He didn't meet me at the door like he usually does."

"He's gotta be here somewhere," Jenny told her soothingly. "You know how he hates storms. He's probably under the bed. Go check."

Renee hurried into their bedroom while Jenny searched David's. No luck. They looked everywhere they could think of in the cabin, but no Fudge.

"Did you remember to lock the doggy door before we left?"

The addition of the small door was something Jenny had

long regretted. All kinds of creatures had made their way into the house before she had eventually realized where they were getting in and had made it a locking door.

"I thought you did."

Jenny gave her a frustrated look. "You know that's your job."

Jenny went to the door and when she twisted the knob, the wind flung it inward, banging it against the wall with such force the panes of glass in the door shattered.

Renee screamed, covering her mouth with her hands.

Pushing against the wind, Jenny went outside, holding on to the rail of the porch, trying to see through the driving rain and darkness.

"Fudge! Here, boy!" The wind seemed to throw the words back in her face. Renee stood framed in the doorway, her anxious eyes trying to peer through the darkness.

"Do you see him?"

"No! Go back inside!"

Jenny called several more times. Where could he be? Already the ground was covered by several inches of water. In the washes and gullies the water would be flowing like a river.

Jenny went back inside, dripping wet. Closing the door, she had to lean against it to get it to shut. The wind whistled eerily through the broken panes of glass in the door, but at least the porch minimized the amount of rain blowing inside. She pushed the wet hair from her eyes, and looked at Renee.

"We'll have to wait for the storm to end, and then we can try to find him."

"But he's out in this! He hates storms. You know he does!" Her voice was increasing in tempo and Jenny could tell she was close to tears.

"Renee, there's nothing we can do right now. It's not safe to be out in this. We'll just have to wait."

Renee turned fearful eyes toward her sister. Her lips

were trembling and tears began falling unheeded down her cheeks.

Teeth chattering, Jenny headed for her bedroom to change. "I need to get out of these wet clothes. See if you can find something to block the wind from coming in those broken panes."

Walking past her sister, Jenny reached out a hand as she went by. Squeezing her shoulder reassuringly, she told her, "He'll be okay."

Jenny wasn't sure who she was trying to comfort more, Renee or herself. Fudge was so small he could easily be swept away by a strong current of water, not to mention the fact that he could very well freeze to death. Where could he have gone, and how long ago did he leave? More than likely, he had been trying to find Renee.

Taking off her wet clothes, she dried herself and put on a pair of jeans and an old sweatshirt. Sitting on the bed, she leaned her face in her hands and offered a brief prayer. *Lord, keep him safe. He's such a little guy.* Her hair was still dripping, so she wrapped it in a towel and returned to the living room.

"Renee, do you want some hot cocoa? I thought I'd fix a snack." Not that she really felt like eating, but it would keep Renee occupied.

When she didn't get an answer, she flipped the towel back and searched the living room. No Renee.

Jenny went swiftly to the kitchen. "Renee? Renee, where are you?"

Surely her sister wouldn't be so foolish as to go out in this. Swallowing panic, she jerked open the kitchen door.

"Renee? Renee!" Rain still pummeled the ground, drowning out the sound of her voice.

There was no answer to her call. Renee had obviously gone in search of Fudge. Jenny hurried outside, scanning the area around her to find some sign of her sister.

"Renee!"

She was nowhere in sight. Fear made it hard for Jenny to think. What should she do? If she went to find her, they could both be lost. She had no idea which direction Renee had gone and neither one of them knew anything about the surrounding area. But neither could she stay here and do nothing. Rubbing her forehead with her hands she tried to reason with herself. *Think. Think. Oh, God! What should I do?*

Choked by fear, she suddenly had a mental picture of Mitch. Of course! Mitch would know what to do. He knew every square inch of this area. Fear for her sister overrode any desire to keep out of his way.

She dashed back inside, hesitating as the lights flickered and then went out.

Jenny groaned. Feeling her way to the living room, she reached for her phone but there was no service. The closest cell tower must have been damaged or else the weather was hindering transmission. A little sob escaped her. *Don't panic. Stay calm.*

Jenny fought the waves of terror threatening to overwhelm her. She needed to get to Mitch. Regardless of the condition of the road, she had to try.

Chapter 14

Mitch was trying to read by the light of a kerosene lamp, but it was useless. His mind was too consumed by thoughts of Jenny.

He hadn't missed the fact that she had quickly ducked out after the ceremony, probably to avoid seeing him. Dark emotion sent a swift current of heat through his body. She could run all she wanted to, but she couldn't hide forever. Eventually she was going to have to face him. He would give her tonight, but tomorrow was another story.

He was jerked from his thoughts by the sudden pounding on his door. Who on earth would be out in a storm like this? Laying the book aside, he quickly crossed the hall and jerked open the door, his eyes widening in surprise when he saw a bedraggled Jenny standing in front of him. Pulling her quickly inside, he shut the door to block out the cold wind.

"What the dickens are you doing out in this? Are you out of your mind?"

She stared up at him a moment before suddenly bursting into tears. Raising his eyebrows, Mitch hesitated only a moment before wrapping her shivering, wet body in his arms. His hands stroked up and down with a soothing, rhythmic motion. A familiar feeling of déjà vu overcame him.

"Jenny, honey, what is it? What's happened?" he questioned softly.

Clinging to the front of his shirt, she lifted a terrified face to his. Through chattering teeth she told him, "Renee's out there!"

Mitch went suddenly still.

"What do you mean 'out there'? In the car?"

"No!" She thumped his chest softly with her fist, as though trying to encourage him to understand. "She went out to find Fudge."

Mitch pulled back from her, gripping her shoulders. His heart was pounding wildly in his chest.

"You mean now? In this storm?"

Jenny could only nod her head.

"Oh, God!" The words were a cry from the soul. Those two words were all Mitch could think to utter and yet they encompassed all the prayers he could have possibly recited.

"Listen to me, Jenny." He shook her gently to make sure he had her full attention. "I'm going to look for her. I want you to stay here. Do you understand me?"

Her eyes widened and she clutched his arm.

"I want to go with you."

"No!" Seeing her distress, he softened his voice. "Listen to me. I need to take a horse. It's too dangerous to be walking and I wouldn't get very far in the Jeep."

"I still want to go," she told him stubbornly. "I know how to ride."

"Listen. I know the territory around here. I'm familiar with the terrain. Regardless, it will still be dangerous wandering around in this kind of weather, for me as well as my horse. I won't risk two horses. Do you understand me?"

Mitch could see the panic in her eyes. Frankly, he knew just how she was feeling but he wasn't about to add his own fear for Jenny into the mix. She would be safer here; knowing that would help him to focus on searching for Renee.

He brushed the tears from her cheeks before bending his head and gently kissing her on the mouth. "Promise me you'll stay put."

Jenny could only nod. No sound could bypass the fear clutching her throat.

She followed Mitch to the door. He pulled on his sheepskin jacket and his Stetson.

Giving her a brief look, he told her, "You need to get out of those wet clothes. My mother's clothes are still in the second bedroom. You should be able to find something that will fit." He disappeared quickly into the darkness.

The rain had lessened, but Jenny knew the danger was far from over. Torrential rains caused flash floods. Pictures of Renee, Fudge and Mitch being swept away filled her mind. Renee was a strong swimmer, but even cars couldn't withstand the rushing water of a flash flood. Groaning, she went to do as Mitch suggested, praying harder than she had ever prayed in her life.

Time continued to tick away and Jenny paced the floor, twisting her hands in frustration. If anyone could find Renee, it was Mitch. But where were they? Had Mitch found her yet? Renee would be devastated if something happened to Fudge. Her chaotic thoughts circled 'round and 'round.

The flickering kerosene lamps gave a mysterious quality to the room. Shadows danced playfully on the walls, mesmerizing in their choreography. At least Mitch had been prepared when the lights went out.

The windup clock on the mantel sounded out with ten chimes. Had it really been three hours since she had arrived? Shouldn't Mitch have found Renee by now? *In pitch darkness,* she chided herself. She pushed her palms against her temples to try to stop the terrifying thoughts. *Dear God, please keep them safe.*

She sank into the armchair beside the sofa, rubbing the back of her neck. A sound from the porch sent her to her feet and flying toward the door. Flinging it open, her hand went to her throat when she saw Mitch standing there with Renee in his arms. Lightning briefly lit the sky in the distance, but thankfully the rain had stopped.

Jenny looked fearfully into his eyes. "Is she all right?"

Mitch pushed past her, heading for the bathroom.

"So far. She's chilled clear through." He lowered Renee onto the chair in the bathroom. "Take over," he told Jenny. "I'll get her one of my mother's robes. Get her out of these wet things and dry her off."

Jenny wrapped her arms around Renee, who was shivering uncontrollably.

"Come on, sweetie, we need to get these wet things off."

A thump on the door told her that Mitch had returned.

"The stuff's in the hall here when you're ready." Jenny could hear him striding away and knew that he would be seeing to his horse before he thought of himself.

Although Delores's clothes were much too big for Renee, Jenny found something that would suit. After getting her dry, Jenny bundled her out to the kitchen. She warmed some milk and made her some cocoa.

Mitch came in, shaking water from his hat. He glanced from one to the other.

"W-h-h-ere's Fudge?" Renee asked him through chattering teeth.

"He's in the barn with the horses. I dried him off and gave him some food and told him to stay. He'll be fine."

"Can't I h-h-have him here w-w-with me?"

Mitch hesitated before nodding. "Sure." He walked across the room and laid a hand on her shoulder. "You need to be in bed. You can use the guest room." His look lingered on Jenny, but then he abruptly turned away. "I'll bring in the pup. The road's a mess. I'd rather you wait till daylight to go home."

"All right, Mitch," Jenny told him quietly. "Thanks."

He glanced at her again, obviously surprised by her acquiescence. Turning, he quickly exited the room.

Jenny helped Renee into bed. When Mitch brought Fudge in, the dog coiled against Renee's legs, his body still trembling. Renee was asleep almost before her head hit the pillow, her damp curls spread out in a fan. One hand lay curled into Fudge's still-damp fur. Watching her, Jenny could hardly breathe through the choking lump in her throat. *Thank You, Lord!*

By the time she returned to the living room, Mitch was there. He had changed clothes; his hair twisting damply against his neck. He motioned her to the couch.

"Have a seat."

Jenny ran her tongue across her lips and cleared her throat. Now that the drama was over, Jenny wasn't sure what to say.

"Thanks."

Polite strangers. Surely after all they had been through together they had gotten past that.

Instead of sitting across from her as he usually did, Mitch took a seat next to her, scattering her composure to the four winds. He leaned back and spread his arms across the back of the couch. It was always impossible to think clearly when he was this near. She always wound up saying something she shouldn't. She tensed, feeling his eyes on her.

"I wanted to thank you for finding Renee," Jenny told him quietly. "I can't ever repay you. I'll never be able to thank you enough."

It was several moments before Mitch answered.

"Renee told me some interesting things while we were out there."

Jenny's eyes flew to his. "Such as?"

"Oh, such as the fact that your hospital stay pretty much wiped out your savings."

Hot color flooded her cheeks. "She had no right."

"That's why you wanted me to buy your ranch. Why couldn't you just tell me?"

Jenny turned away, but Mitch leaned forward, taking her face in his hands. Her heart started beating faster as his green eyes plumbed the depths of her blue ones.

"She also told me about some fool of a guy named Alexander."

Jenny's eyes went wide. "How could she possibly have known about him? I never told anyone except my mother."

Mitch smiled, but he remained serious. "Little pitchers have big ears, as the saying goes. She overheard a conversation between you and your mother."

Jenny shook her head. "She never said anything."

Mitch softly stroked a finger over her lip. "Honey, if he couldn't see what a gem you are, he was totally blind."

The feelings that overtook her at that statement left her helpless against his charisma. What exactly was he trying to say?

"I want you to tell me something. Honestly. Will you do that?" he asked.

Jenny wasn't sure what was coming, but she nodded. What did it matter if he knew about her finances now, anyway?

"Do you love me?"

Her eyes widened in surprise and she would have turned away again but he wouldn't let her.

"You said you would answer honestly," he said.

She sucked in a breath and let it expire on a soft sigh. She was so very tired of pretending.

"Yes," she told him, dropping her lashes.

"Jenny," he breathed tenderly, his strong arms wrapping securely around her. Her lashes flew upward and she watched a slow smile spread itself across his handsome face. That same smile that always rocked her insides. His lips came down on hers gently at first, the pressure suddenly increasing when she offered no resistance.

For Jenny, the whole world seemed to have stopped spinning and left her behind. Could it be true, what Mitch's lips were telling her? What about Amanda? Pushing away, she put as much distance between them as he would allow.

"Wait a minute. What about Amanda?"

He sighed. "I just knew that was what you were thinking."

"I saw you together at the funeral, and then you left town with her."

Mitch smiled as he looked down at her.

"Do you know you have the cutest pout? Every time I see that bottom lip stick out, I get this overwhelming desire to kiss you." Suiting the action to the words, he kissed her briefly, his eyes alight with humor.

Jenny stared back at him, eyes flashing.

"Don't try to change the subject. What about Amanda?" The fire left her as quickly as it had come. "She's so beautiful."

"Trust me. Her beauty is only skin-deep. Whereas yours…" He paused and hot color flooded her face at his look.

"I'm well aware of what I look like."

"Are you? Are you, my little Jenny Wren?" He forced her to look him in the eye. "You have a beauty that transcends the physical. It's something I can't even begin to put into words. Just trust me when I say that to me you're the most beautiful woman in the world. And I didn't leave town with Amanda. She just happened to leave at the same time. She went her way and I went mine."

Surely this was a dream and she would wake up to find herself back in her bedroom at the cabin. "But at the funeral…"

"Can we just forget about Amanda?" he growled in frustration. "I made it quite clear to her that I was in love with someone else."

"You did? I mean, you are?"

He shook his head, grinning unabashedly at her. "We've wasted a lot of time, my darling," he told her. "If it hadn't been for a few misunderstandings, we could have been married by now."

"Married? You want to marry me?"

She knew she must sound like an absolute dolt, but she couldn't get her mind to function logically. She had allowed one experience with a man to color her thinking and she was having a hard time letting go of that past and looking forward to the future.

A flame seemed to ignite in the depths of Mitch's eyes, turning them a deep emerald. What she saw there turned her bones to jelly. As hard as it was to believe, Jenny knew for sure that Mitch truly loved her.

"I don't understand," she said. "If you wanted to marry me, why didn't you say something?"

Mitch leaned back, pulling Jenny with him. He kept his arms firmly wrapped around her as though he were afraid she might disappear. Curling her head into his shoulder, she nestled against him.

"Jenny, Jenny." He sighed, staring off into space, gathering his thoughts together. "I wasn't particularly anxious to get involved with you." He felt her stiffen. "As you know, I didn't have much faith in women. Only after my mother came back…only then did I realize how selfish and arrogant I had been, expecting everyone to live up to *my* ideals. But it wasn't until I almost lost you forever that I realized just how much I cared. I was going to ask you to marry me the minute you got out of the hospital, but then my mother…"

He hesitated and she finished the thought for him. "Your

mother was sick." Sighing, Jenny leaned her head back and looked up at him. "I liked your mother."

A wry half smile tilted Mitch's lips. "I liked the woman she became."

He glanced down at her, his eyes trailing a path across her face.

"But then after the accident, you changed and Hattie told me I needed to give you time."

Jenny buried her head against his shoulder, remembering those turbulent events.

"Then you asked me to buy your ranch and I was more confused than ever."

"I was just as confused. I lacked the faith to believe God could take care of us. I forgot for a time just how much He had done for us already. I was ashamed of myself for being such a coward. And I was afraid that you would think I was after your money if I continued to see you."

The silence lengthened. Mitch was the first to break it.

"So, will you?"

Lost in her dreams, Jenny wasn't certain what he was asking.

"Hmm? Will I what?"

Grinning, he caught her chin between his thumb and fingers to catch her full attention.

"Will you marry me?"

"In a heartbeat," she told him softly.

Mitch laughed then bent to kiss her and they were lost in a world of their own.

* * * * *

REQUEST YOUR FREE BOOKS!

2 FREE INSPIRATIONAL NOVELS
PLUS 2
FREE
MYSTERY GIFTS

Love Inspired

YES! Please send me 2 FREE Love Inspired® novels and my 2 FREE mystery gifts (gifts are worth about $10). After receiving them, if I don't wish to receive any more books, I can return the shipping statement marked "cancel." If I don't cancel, I will receive 6 brand-new novels every month and be billed just $4.74 per book in the U.S. or $5.24 per book in Canada. That's a savings of at least 21% off the cover price. It's quite a bargain! Shipping and handling is just 50¢ per book in the U.S. and 75¢ per book in Canada.* I understand that accepting the 2 free books and gifts places me under no obligation to buy anything. I can always return a shipment and cancel at any time. Even if I never buy another book, the two free books and gifts are mine to keep forever.

105/305 IDN F49N

Name	(PLEASE PRINT)	

Address		Apt. #

City	State/Prov.	Zip/Postal Code

Signature (if under 18, a parent or guardian must sign)

Mail to the Harlequin® Reader Service:
IN U.S.A.: P.O. Box 1867, Buffalo, NY 14240-1867
IN CANADA: P.O. Box 609, Fort Erie, Ontario L2A 5X3

**Are you a subscriber to Love Inspired books
and want to receive the larger-print edition?
Call 1-800-873-8635 or visit www.ReaderService.com.**

* Terms and prices subject to change without notice. Prices do not include applicable taxes. Sales tax applicable in N.Y. Canadian residents will be charged applicable taxes. Offer not valid in Quebec. This offer is limited to one order per household. Not valid for current subscribers to Love Inspired books. All orders subject to credit approval. Credit or debit balances in a customer's account(s) may be offset by any other outstanding balance owed by or to the customer. Please allow 4 to 6 weeks for delivery. Offer available while quantities last.

Your Privacy—The Harlequin® Reader Service is committed to protecting your privacy. Our Privacy Policy is available online at www.ReaderService.com or upon request from the Harlequin Reader Service.
We make a portion of our mailing list available to reputable third parties that offer products we believe may interest you. If you prefer that we not exchange your name with third parties, or if you wish to clarify or modify your communication preferences, please visit us at www.ReaderService.com/consumerchoice or write to us at Harlequin Reader Service Preference Service, P.O. Box 9062, Buffalo, NY 14269. Include your complete name and address.

REQUEST YOUR FREE BOOKS!

2 FREE INSPIRATIONAL NOVELS
PLUS 2
FREE
MYSTERY GIFTS

Love Inspired

HISTORICAL
INSPIRATIONAL HISTORICAL ROMANCE

YES! Please send me 2 FREE Love Inspired® Historical novels and my 2 FREE mystery gifts (gifts are worth about $10). After receiving them, if I don't wish to receive any more books, I can return the shipping statement marked "cancel." If I don't cancel, I will receive 4 brand-new novels every month and be billed just $4.74 per book in the U.S. or $5.24 per book in Canada. That's a savings of at least 21% off the cover price. It's quite a bargain! Shipping and handling is just 50¢ per book in the U.S. and 75¢ per book in Canada.* I understand that accepting the 2 free books and gifts places me under no obligation to buy anything. I can always return a shipment and cancel at any time. Even if I never buy another book, the two free books and gifts are mine to keep forever.

102/302 IDN F5CY

Name	(PLEASE PRINT)	
Address		Apt. #
City	State/Prov.	Zip/Postal Code

Signature (if under 18, a parent or guardian must sign)

Mail to the **Harlequin®** Reader Service:
IN U.S.A.: P.O. Box 1867, Buffalo, NY 14240-1867
IN CANADA: P.O. Box 609, Fort Erie, Ontario L2A 5X3

Want to try two free books from another series?
Call 1-800-873-8635 or visit www.ReaderService.com.

* Terms and prices subject to change without notice. Prices do not include applicable taxes. Sales tax applicable in N.Y. Canadian residents will be charged applicable taxes. Offer not valid in Quebec. This offer is limited to one order per household. Not valid for current subscribers to Love Inspired Historical books. All orders subject to credit approval. Credit or debit balances in a customer's account(s) may be offset by any other outstanding balance owed by or to the customer. Please allow 4 to 6 weeks for delivery. Offer available while quantities last.

Your Privacy—The Harlequin® Reader Service is committed to protecting your privacy. Our Privacy Policy is available online at www.ReaderService.com or upon request from the Harlequin Reader Service.

We make a portion of our mailing list available to reputable third parties that offer products we believe may interest you. If you prefer that we not exchange your name with third parties, or if you wish to clarify or modify your communication preferences, please visit us at www.ReaderService.com/consumerschoice or write to us at Harlequin Reader Service Preference Service, P.O. Box 9062, Buffalo, NY 14269. Include your complete name and address.

LIHDIR13R

ReaderService.com

Manage your account online!

- Review your order history
- Manage your payments
- Update your address

*We've designed
the Harlequin® Reader Service
website just for you.*

Enjoy all the features!

- Reader excerpts from any series
- Respond to mailings and special monthly offers
- Discover new series available to you
- Browse the Bonus Bucks catalog
- Share your feedback

Visit us at:

ReaderService.com